SPLIT

STAND UP. BE SEEN. BREAK OUT.

This World Book Day 2020 book is
a gift from your local bookseller and
Macmillan Children's Books

#ShareAStory

CELEBRATE STORIES. LOVE READING.

This book has been specially created and published to celebrate **World Book Day**. World Book Day is a charity funded by publishers and booksellers in the UK and Ireland. Our mission is to offer every child and young person the opportunity to read and love books by giving you the chance to have a book of your own. To find out more, and get great recommendations on what to read next, visit **worldbookday.com**

World Book Day in the UK and Ireland is also made possible by generous sponsorship from National Book Tokens and support from authors and illustrators.

World Book Day works in partnership with a number of charities, who are all working to encourage a love of reading for pleasure.

BookTrust is the UK's largest children's reading charity. Each year we reach 3.4 million children across the UK with books, resources and support to help develop a love of reading. **booktrust.org.uk**

The National Literacy Trust is an independent charity that encourages children and young people to enjoy reading. Just 10 minutes of reading every day can make a big difference to how well you do at school and to how successful you could be in life. **literacytrust.org.uk**

The Reading Agency inspires people of all ages and backgrounds to read for pleasure and empowerment. They run the Summer Reading Challenge in partnership with libraries; they also support reading groups in schools and libraries all year round. Find out more and join your local library. **summerreadingchallenge. org.uk**

World Book Day also facilitates fundraising for:

Book Aid International, an international book donation and library development charity. Every year, they provide one million books to libraries and schools in communities where children would otherwise have little or no opportunity to read. **bookaid.org**

Read for Good, who motivate children in schools to read for fun through its sponsored read, which thousands of schools run on World Book Day and throughout the year. The money raised provides new books and resident storytellers in all the children's hospitals in the UK. **readforgood.org**

Also by Muhammad Khan
from Macmillan Children's Books

I Am Thunder
Kick the Moon

Coming soon
Mark My Words

SPLIT

STAND UP. BE SEEN. BREAK OUT.

MUHAMMAD KHAN

MACMILLAN

First published 2020 by Macmillan Children's Books
an imprint of Pan Macmillan
The Smithon, 6 Briset Street, London, EC1M 5NR
Associated companies throughout the world
www.panmacmillan.com

ISBN 978-1-5290-3923-8

1 3 5 7 9 8 6 4 2

A CIP catalogue record for this book is available from the British Library.
Printed and bound by CPI Group (UK) Ltd, Croydon CR0 4YY
Holmen Paper Ltd and Gould Paper Sales UK Ltd contributed towards
the production of this title printed on 52gsm Holmen Bulky

To all the special young people who inspired Salma and Billie.

Keep doing you.

Happy World Book Day!

#CastingCall #Audition #MusicalTheatre

Attention: We are casting for a girl 15–19 to star in a groundbreaking adaption of CINDERELLA.

This is an open call to audition before Olivier and Tony Award-winning judge Edwina Hirsch!

Candidates <u>must have experience of acting and singing</u> (dancing is desirable). A superb opportunity to break into theatre, film and television. More details on our website. Please complete the form online.

Auditions to be held on July 1st.

Prepare a classic monologue and any song you feel represents Cinderella's plight.

Fortuna Theatre
13 Rollins Street

PROLOGUE

'Cinderella audition tape: take one.'

I cough because my vocal chords were not designed for busting out such gravelly bass tones. The coughing fit morphs into a cussing fit. Suddenly aware of the camera again, I slap a hand over my mouth – if I'm going to win the judges over, I've gotta be less Gordon Ramsay and more My Little Pony. *Ah, screw it!* I delete the video, setting my phone back on the window ledge for take two.

Our poky lounge is my recording studio, the one room in our house that doesn't look like a tornado hit it. Even when Dad was alive, we weren't exactly rolling in money, but for some reason we've always had way too much stuff. Ten boot sales worth of tat squished inside a two-bedroom house. Thank God I'm not claustrophobic. I glance at my watch. Got an hour forty-five before my first ever date. I'm nervous as hell but Tariq seems pretty chill. I made it *completely* clear that Netflix and dinner is in no way the same as 'Netflix and Chill'. Our evening will be strictly PG and if he can prove he's not some pervy *goonda*, there may be a follow-up appointment.

'Take two!' I say, making a cutesy peace sign. 'Thanks for having me. Honestly, I'm trying so hard not to fangirl right now. Ms Hirsch, I can't believe it's actually you. You're my acting inspo.'

OK, less arse-kissing, more auditioning!

'So, anyway, my name's Salma Hashmi.' I frown, wondering whether to move straight on to take three. 'Make that just Salma. My surname belonged to my dad and, well, it's complicated.'

Why did I even bring Dad up? He's dead, buried, gone forever – which is exactly why I now get to try out for this role. I rub my temples, trying to remember what's next on my prompt sheet instead of focusing on my disapproving departed dad. Casting directors are busy people. You got twenty seconds to knock it out of the park or you're going home.

'I'm fifteen and from Haringey. All my life I've wanted to be an actress.' Lame. 'You probably get that a lot, huh? But for me . . . look, good stuff doesn't happen to people like me. It don't matter how much talent you got, nobody gives you a chance. They take one look at you and they think they got you sussed.'

Wow. I'm in a whole other postcode from the

script. The camera's running but I suddenly feel I need to say the words that have been sitting inside me like broken glass. Better to get it out now than in the actual audition.

'I just want a chance to show the world what I can do. I know I look nothing like the Cinderella in your head but I'm going to prove that I can be ten times better. Talk is cheap and time is money. You asked for a song, so here it is. Enjoy.'

My song choice is 'Somewhere Over the Rainbow'. Apart from boasting a bulletproof melody and sentimental Cinderella vibes, it speaks to me on a whole bunch of levels, about hoping for a better life and being frustrated with the hoops and hurdles between you and your dreams. I know there are people in my community who think acting is all kinds of evil, just like Dad did, but I'm done caring. Drama is the only thing I'm good at and I'm not going to be ashamed of it.

Inhaling deeply, I open my mouth and out drifts a lilting lullaby. So far so good – maybe even great? But let's not hold a party just yet cos if life's taught me one thing, it's that karma comes for show-offs. So I get a grip, remembering to sing from the diaphragm, working my way up to the top note. My core temperature rises and I can *feel* it happening, like me and Adele just got body-swapped. Excited butterflies flutter in my belly, beating their wings faster and faster and—

My voice cracks.

What should have been a showstopping power note comes off like a squirrel's fart. I collapse back onto the settee, cringing. Kill me now.

CHAPTER 1

The date was the biggest disaster of my life. I'm not even lying. Cannot handle school today after the humiliation of last night but Mum's on the warpath, so I better not push it. Frankly, it's a miracle I haven't already been kicked out.

The sun beats down like it's mad at me too, making me sweat so bad I feel like a basted chicken. I pop into the bakery on the way to school to buy a pink slice of sickly sweet cake. That much sugar could make the wicked stepmother crack a smile. The shop assistant tells me they're on offer so I grab an extra slice for my best mate, Muzna. We've been tight forever: literally born on the same day and in the very same hospital. Muzna's parents have always been proper strict, trying to raise her as the perfect Pakistani daughter. I'm perfect nothing, but it ain't for lack of Dad trying.

Muzna thinks I lucked out with high cheekbones and big eyes. Those things might be Insta currency, but likes won't buy you a bigger house or get you a good job. Muzna's always getting top marks in class and has something smart to say. That's the kind of stuff you can build a life on. Pretty isn't forever.

When I get to school on the one day I need to pour my heart out the most, Muzna is nowhere to be found. Smirks and whispers surround me like fog, hounding my every step. Somehow everyone already knows about the date.

'Hey,' says a ginger kid, a football balanced under his arm. 'Wanna visit *my* bedroom after school?' He flicks his tongue in a way that makes me want to punch his lights out.

'Say that again, see what happens,' I warn.

He backs off, warily eyeing my clenched fist. The rumours have started and it's not even 9 a.m.

At lunchtime, I finally corner Muzna in the dinner hall and I go to hug her, but she just bursts into tears and runs off, dumping her lunch in the bin. Muzna and me do not dump food in bins. We can't afford to.

A folded sheet of pink paper by the bin catches my eye. Even before I've opened it, my heart's taken the lift down to the basement of my soul. It's from Muzna, begging me to understand that her parents will kill her if she's seen with me after what happened last night.

I knew her parents were mad but I didn't expect her to do *this*. Tariq screwed up and *I* get blamed.

A boy wolf whistles behind me and I whip round with a glare freshly baked in the fires of hell. 'Easy, fam!' he says. 'Tariq said he hit all the bases last night. *A home run on a first date!'*

Tariq, I decide, needs his jaw wired shut. He's by the lockers now, boasting to a crowd of pervy boys, making graphic gestures that leave me in no doubt what he's on about. They see me coming and undress me with their eyes.

'Gotta go! Bye!' Tariq says bouncing.

'Oi! You get your lying arse back here!' I feel my skirt snag on something and spin round as a boy tries to lift it. I kick his phone out of his other hand so hard the screen has cracked before it even hits the floor.

'You're paying for that!' he shrieks as I pelt down the corridor after Tariq.

Longer legs and a head start give him an advantage, but outrage spikes my adrenalin and soon enough I'm honing in on the idiot like a BS-seeking missile. Tariq makes the mistake of looking back once too often and runs straight into a 'CLEANING IN PROGRESS' sign. Feet tangling, arms pinwheeling, he hits the floor and rolls over. I land on him in a straddle, slamming into his belly with the force of an Anthony Joshua uppercut. Groaning, he grips my wrists before I do any real damage.

'Why you spreading lies about me?' I demand, fingers twitching.

'I didn't!' he says. 'I told them we spent last night together. It's the truth!'

'He did more than tell us,' laughs a kid. Tariq looks daggers at him, shaking his head furiously. The kid continues undeterred. 'My boy posted pics on Insta!'

Another kid, one I actually thought liked me, holds up a phone and my heart implodes. In the pic I'm asleep on a bed, but Tariq is posed behind me, bare shoulders and torso emerging from a duvet giving a cheesy thumbs up. One swipe later and my cheeks are burning. The next picture is of Tariq licking the side of my face like it's made of chocolate. They say the camera never lies but this one ain't telling the whole story.

'*Why would you do that*?' The betrayal makes me gasp.

'Ain't my fault you're so easy.' Wrong answer.

My fist connects with his jaw, whipping his face to the left with an audible crack.

'Raaa! Tariq got Me-Tooed,' quips some idiot in the crowd that's started to gather now there's a real fight on.

'Don't ever come at me with your BS again!' I yell into his face. 'Understand?'

He cowers. Point made, I get off him and turn to walk away.

'Salma's gonna be a movie star, y'all!' Tariq yells behind me, humiliating me with the one needle of truth in a haystack of lies. He makes me wish so hard I hadn't shown him my audition tape – why did I ever think I could trust him? Just cos he boo-hooed about his parents getting divorced? 'Reckons she's gonna be the new Cinderella.'

Shut up! Shut up! But he keeps right on, laying my soul bare for the entire world to laugh at.

'Yeah, riiiiight!' say the vicious glamour queens in disgust.

Once upon time, these three figured I was pretty

enough to join their clique. Strutting round the school, ordering other students about like servants – it was a proposal nobody in their right mind would reject. But then they made the mistake of picking on Muzna for having too much facial hair. Muzzie's super sensitive about stuff like that and I was done with their meanness. So I ditched them and they've haunted me ever since. Muzna wouldn't let them get to me, told me that school wasn't forever and that my acting talent would take me places.

But now I've lost Muzna and this boy is the reason.

'The only movie you'll be seeing Salma in,' Tariq continues, a grin splitting his face, 'is the kind that gets passed around the boys' locker room!'

Howls of laugher and 'Raa!' swell around us, trapping me in an inescapable dome of humiliation.

The sympathy I felt for Tariq over his parents' divorce burns in the inferno of my rage. I turn again, grabbing a fire extinguisher and lifting it over my head. Tariq's left me with zero chill and is about to find out why that was such a big mistake.

'Stop that right now!' roars Mrs Roche, our Head of Year.

Problem is: *I can't*. Floating five metres in the air, looking down on the scene, is the real me, as shook as everyone else. Down on the ground is feral Salma — the one Tariq's lies created — preparing to teach him a lesson.

One of Tariq's mates rips the fire extinguisher out of my hands while Mrs Roche yanks me backwards. Reflexively I round on her, snarling, ready to take a chunk out of her throat. Then just like that, two Salmas become one and I rein it in.

'Come with me to the head teacher's office. Now!' Roche growls.

'Bet she's an animal in the sack an' all!' says a boy, making the assembly of onlookers double up in hysterics.

'Cinderella?' the mean girls scoff. 'More like Skankerella. What a total slut!'

CHAPTER 2

Mrs Fossey looks at me with savage distaste.

'What?' I say, splaying my fingers. 'It weren't my fault.'

'Half the school witnessed you attacking Tariq, not to mention it was captured on CCTV.' She holds up her phone. I wince, looking at the paused image.

'OK, so I admit it looks bad, but I was *provoked*. The boy's been spreading rumours.'

'And you think that justifies a violent response?'

'You don't understand. My reputation is destroyed.'

'You roll your skirt ten centimetres shorter than regulation length. You wear false eyelashes and a bright red lipstick—'

'It's red-orange with UV protection,' I point out.

'Which is in direct contravention to school rules. You don't seem to be doing anything to dissuade this reputation you speak of,' Fossey says tartly.

I blink, totally shocked by her attitude. Just cos Fossey's happy looking like a walrus fart doesn't mean the rest of us should be dissed for making an effort. 'I'm telling you, I was *provoked*! I'm not a violent person, you can ask anyone!'

'Provoked into physically assaulting a boy who took a picture of you two together?' My mouth falls open, blood rushing to my face. 'Yes, I know all about *that*. A parent called in this morning to complain. Your behaviour has brought the entire school into disrepute.'

'Speak to Tariq. He's the one posting fake pictures.'

'I understand you're upset and we shall get to the bottom of Tariq's behaviour but violence is never the answer. This is a very serious matter, Salma. I'm going to have to call your mother in.'

'No! You can't!' I cry, my hand wrapping round her wrist, stopping her from lifting the telephone off its cradle. Her hooded lids retract, like a poisonous reptile queen who is about to attack.

I. Am. So. Dead.

Mum drives me home. She's vexed.

'Mum?'

Silence.

'Mummy?'

'Just be quiet, please, Salma,' her voice rasps, puffy bags swelling under her eyes. 'I'm struggling to understand how I could've raised you so wrong.'

'You didn't!' I assure her. 'You taught me to stand up for my rights, which I did. Before you came, Mrs Fossey was saying all this crap, making out I'm the one to blame instead of Tariq.'

'Maybe you're both to blame.'

Oof! 'Mum, are you serious?'

'I gave you all the freedom my parents never gave me,' she says tearing up, her voice trembling. 'In the past twenty-four hours you've single-handedly managed to make yourself look like a wild child and me like a terrible mother. There are scandalous pictures of you on the internet, Salma! That never goes away! And as if that isn't terrible enough, you get a two-week exclusion for fighting.'

'I didn't mean to—'

'Do you have any idea how hard I work in A&E to look after us? Hmm, do you?' I sink lower in the seat. 'I do day shifts, I do night shifts, I work with drunks and thugs who hurl abuse at me till they're blue in the face. They call me worse things than what that stupid boy called you.'

When Dad was alive, I got to blame him for all the bad things that ever happened to us. But who do I blame now? Mum's burdened with a daughter who keeps getting in trouble no matter how many sacrifices she makes for me. I'd do anything to make it up to her but how do I turn back time? Why did Tariq — my first date ever — have to turn out to be such a jerk?

'I'm sorry, Mum.' I mean it for every bit of pain or disappointment I've ever caused her.

Mum's lips stitch together, smothering a harsh comeback — one which I totally deserve. I wonder if every time she looks at me, she sees Dad staring back. People always called me 'Daddy's Girl'. Could I be just as messed up in the head as he was? Even if I'm *not* like him, one thing is clear: I'm no better for Mum than Dad ever was.

CHAPTER 3

Looking back on it, I'm not even sure why I agreed to go on the date with Tariq. Not to sound up myself but I've had way better offers and each time I turned them down. Then Tariq came along, this nerdy little try hard. He wasn't like the others who'd tell me how hot I was or what they'd like to do to me. Tariq was clumsy but at least he actually tried to talk to me. Made me laugh; made me feel sorry for him. I guess I believed it was something in my life that was mine, that I could control.

'Wanna come round my place?' he'd asked hopefully in the corridor at lunchtime. He was pretending to be cool but his hands were bare shaking. When he quickly stuffed them in his pockets, it made me smile.

'You mean for a date?'

'Yeah, yeah. My uncle's given me a house, like for when I'm eighteen, innit? We can watch Netflix on the massive seventy-five inch 8K def TV.' His arms spread wide, fingers splayed, as if the TV screen was the size of a bus. 'And we can do dinner.'

'Riiiight,' I say. 'Then we can take your uncle's private jet to Honolulu and hire Ed Sheeran to play ukulele while we stuff our faces with caviar.'

'I ain't lying!'

'I'm seeing Muzna tonight anyway.'

'What that girl with the 'tache?'

'Why does everybody do that? She's my best mate and I don't appreciate you knocking her.'

'Sorry! Sorry!' he said, raising his hands in apology. 'I don't know her, innit? I only go by what other people chat.'

I should have stopped it right there. His statement was a big red flag with bells on. But the pips went and I needed to get to maths. He followed me all the way there, begging and pleading. He made me feel like a queen and you know what? Flattery can make the sanest people do the dumbest things. So I agreed to swing by later, squeeze him in before a sleepover at Muzna's.

At 6 p.m. I found myself standing outside a tall house on a posh street. As I rechecked Google maps, the front door opened, the porch light illuminating Tariq's desperate grin. 'You made it! Sweet.'

He said the TV was up in the master bedroom.

'You for real? I've just stepped in your place and you're already trying to get me in your bedroom.'

He panicked. 'Swear down the TV's in the bedroom! It belongs to my uncle. Look, I'll level with you: this house isn't really mine. My uncle's a property developer. He's looking for high-end tenants for this place. He ain't found them yet so I thought we could have a fun evening.' He swallowed, his Adam's apple pogoing up and down his skinny throat. 'Sometimes I come here when I want to get away from stuff.'

'What stuff?'

'My parents.' Well that was blunt. 'They're always arguing, innit?'

With the saddest look on his face, he told me his parents were getting divorced and they were traumatizing him with their twenty-four-seven shouting matches. It scared him, made him angry and helpless. His little brother had him to tell lies about everything being OK. But Tariq had no one. 'They reckon cos I'm nearly sixteen, I'm a big man, innit? And I don't got feelings. Their stupid, selfish problems are doing my head in.'

We sat on the thickly carpeted stairs, chatting

about family problems. I didn't tell him everything, but I told him enough to know that living with Dad had been a nightmare.

'When he died, it made me realize how short life is. So I'm going to be an actor.' I instantly regretted blabbing. You tell people personal stuff about yourself, you give them power to hurt you.

'You wanna be an actress?' he asked, shaking his head and grinning. 'Well, you're peng enough.'

'You think?'

'Solid eleven. I can imagine you working it in a wet saree.' He started singing some smutty Bollywood song and thrusting his pelvis. I would've been angry but for the fact I unexpectedly started laughing. He looked so damn foolish, hanging on to the stair rail, waggling his eyebrows as he gestured as suggestively as a Nautch dancing girl. We both cracked up and somehow it made me feel relaxed – brought my protective barrier down.

Tariq asked why it was so important for me to see Muzna later.

'She's helping me learn lines for my audition,' I explained.

'You're serious about this.' Tariq said, the penny

finally dropping. 'You don't mind all the uncle-*jis* and the auntie-*jis* chatting crap about you?'

'What do you mean?'

'Well cos acting is basically lying. You're pretending something that ain't is true. Plus you have to kiss all those men, do nude scenes, hop into bed with ugly old film producers . . .'

'I ain't doing no nudes—'

He suddenly pushed his lips up against mine. It was a sloppy kiss but I allowed it. 'You know, you're a good kisser.'

'Yeah, well, you ain't.' It felt exactly like having a warm jelly shoved in my face.

'Let me try again . . .'

'Maybe later,' I said, hurriedly getting up. 'Plus, don't just kiss a girl, bruv. Ask first. You get me?'

He pulled a face. 'OK, OK. May I please kiss you, Miss Beautiful Bollywood Goddessness?'

I scowled. 'So just cos I'm Asian means Bollywood is my only option?'

He licked his lips. 'OK, so can I kiss you Miss Holly-Bolly-Lolly-Jolly-Wood?'

Somehow he'd done it again. I was in hysterics.

'So, when's your audition?'

I told him it was tomorrow and he offered to let me practise my monologue with him. He even agreed to film it so I could fine-tune my performance later.

'You deserve an Oscar!' he said enthusiastically after my fifth take.

I thanked him then wrinkled my nose. 'I'm hungry. Where's this dinner you promised?'

He grinned. 'On it. Why don't you go check out the TV?'

I gave him a look but he was already opening up a food app on his phone to order in, so I went upstairs to see if the bus-sized TV really existed. The master bedroom was super classy, decorated in subtle creams, with a king-size bed, but my eyes were drawn to the opposite wall where a TV, almost as big as the screen down the local cinema, was fixed to the wall. So Tariq wasn't lying. I hesitated for no more than five seconds before grabbing the remote and channel surfing and finally settling on *Glee*. The picture quality made me feel like I was sinking into the TV and the sound seemed to be seeping out of the walls. I wasn't just singing along but singing *with* my favourite characters, fully immersed in the action.

Tariq came in and instead of calling me out for being cringey, he grabbed a can of air freshener for a mic and joined me up on the bed-stage. We bopped like it was 1995. I was living my best life.

We both collapsed onto the bed, sweaty, dizzy but still buzzing.

'Man, that was so fun!' Tariq said, mopping his brow. 'Look: actual sweat! I keep this up, I'm going to get a six-pack.'

'Now imagine doing this as a job for life. Getting paid to have fun. That's how I feel about acting,' I explained.

'Yeah but most actors don't sing and dance though.'

'You do if you're auditioning for musical theatre.'

He rolled over, placing a hand on my thigh. 'You didn't say nothing about that.'

I sat up, discreetly slipping free of his wandering hand. 'Cos I thought you'd take the piss. But you're actually kinda chill.'

'I'll take it, though I would've preferred sexy. So what role you up for?' He sits up, casually sliding an arm around me.

I pause for a beat. 'Cinderella. It's a fresh take on the fairy tale.'

'Nice . . .' His hand began wandering again. I promptly caught it.

'Look, Tariq, I like you. A lot, yeah? But we need to take things slower. You get me?'

'But actors always get it on in five minutes!'

'Yeah, cos it's not real. Plus, I already told you, I'm never gonna take roles that make me feel uncomfortable. So . . .' I shrugged my shoulders and shook my head.

The doorbell rang and whatever he might've said in return was forgotten when he came back, arms laden with paper bags. 'Grub's up!'

'Dude, what is this? You promised me a candlelit dinner and you bring me back a bucket of hotwings?'

'This ain't hotwings. This is a fourteen-piece Mela Meal Deal from LFC!'

'Liverpool Football Club?'

'Lahori Fried Chicken-shiken!' he said in an exaggerated accent. 'It's finger *chaat*-ing good!'

You know that feeling you get when you're having a nightmare and you trip so bad your whole body jerks you right awake? We'd eaten so much fried chicken that I'd fallen completely asleep. But the nightmare got ten times worse when I opened my eyes. Seven angry Asian men were crowding round the bed.

'Tariq?' one of them said in surprise, poking him with a baseball bat. 'I brought my friends thinking there'd been a bloody break-in.'

I shrank behind the duvet moments before it was ripped off. Tariq yelped, lanky limbs clamouring to cover himself like a terrorized spider. To my horror he was in his underpants.

'Look, it's that missing girl!' an uncle announced with boggling eyes.

'Shame on you!' one of them said in Urdu. 'Your mother is worried sick wondering where you are and you're sleeping with my nephew!

'Oh my God, this is so not what it looks like!' I told them, breaking out in a sweat. As if it couldn't get any worse, I recognized one of them as Uncle Saleem, Muzna's dad. Knowing him, something would go down with Muzna later. The look in their eyes said it all: nothing that came out of my mouth would ever be the truth. To confirm it, one of them jabbed a finger at me.

'*Besharam*!'

Being called 'shameless' in English is hurtful; having it said in Urdu legit feels like you got disembowelled with a hot poker.

Mum passed down the line of frowning uncles, avoiding their eyes, like it was a walk of shame. Apparently, they'd been out looking for me after I failed to answer Mum's calls. Then they got a call from Tariq's uncle, freaking out over what he figured was a break-in. Wary of the police, they'd decided to handle the matter themselves.

'Let's go,' Mum said simply.

'Mum, I—'

She turned her back on me, making a beeline for the door. Can't say I blame her.

'Tell them what really happened! *Please*!' I begged Tariq.

Tariq looked at me then pointed at his dad. 'This is your fault! You and Mum. If you loved me, like you're supposed to, I wouldn't look somewhere else.'

'You're blaming me for sleeping with this girl?' Tariq's dad shouted.

Mum whipped around. 'That's my daughter you're talking about!'

The uncles' eyes widened in surprise before Uncle Saleem spoke up. 'Please take Salma home.'

'Oh my days!' I cried, exasperated. 'There was no sleeping! OK? What is wrong with you people? Tariq, I'm begging you: *tell them the truth*.'

Tariq gave me a blank stare, like he had no clue what I was on about.

'Salma!' Mum hollered from the threshold, signalling for me to follow.

Fists balled, I gave a frustrated scream and pointed at Tariq. 'I get blacklisted, I'mma come so hard for you, you'll wish you never messed with me.'

Tariq looked between the faces of the angry men then back at me. 'I already wish I hadn't messed with you. You drew me into temptation.'

My jaw dropped just as Mum, grabbing my arm, hauled me out of that toxic environment and down the front drive.

Mum didn't acknowledge me again until we were safely sealed inside her Corsa with the engine running. The motor sounded like it had a phlegmy cough. 'What happened?'

Not the question I was expecting. It made me want to hug her and thank her for asking me instead of jumping to conclusions. But I was smart enough to know that a move like that could get me in trouble. All around us uncles were getting into their cars, throwing shade on a sliding scale of disgust to outright hatred. I want to give them the finger, but for Mum's sake I didn't.

'I didn't do nothing, Mum,' I stammered. 'Not like what they're saying, anyway.'

'So what exactly were you doing in there with that boy? You told me you were having a sleepover with Muzna.'

'That was the plan. I was going to Muzzie's straight after.'

'I called her. She knew nothing about a sleepover.'

'My phone's dodge. I didn't get a chance to run it by her, but you know she's always up for it.'

'That doesn't explain why you were in bed with him.' Mum gave the signal and pulled out, sidelights punching holes through the dark.

'He wanted to help me prep for my audition tomorrow,' I explain. Not entirely true, but not a flat-out lie either.

'So you jumped into bed with him?'

'No! We were sat on his bed, eating fried chicken, watching Netflix on a massive TV. I think I ate too much. You know that makes you drowsy, right? I fell asleep by accident. That's all. I swear.'

'Don't you realize how dangerous that is? Just falling asleep in some random boy's bedroom?'

'I didn't mean to. He'd already conked out . . . I thought he was trustworthy.' I hold my head, trying to make sense of the madness and betrayal. 'Somewhere between me falling asleep and those uncles turning up, that idiot must have stripped down to his underwear. Aw, Mum, don't cry!'

Fat teardrops rolled down her cheeks. 'I thought you knew better. I told you I didn't want you dating until you're eighteen. We live in a close-knit community, Salma. There are people on our street who hold very tight to their traditional values.'

'Please! Everybody's dating and worse – including kids down our street! Khalil's two-timing Monifa and Zoe, and Auntie Balquis's precious Yasmin is always posting two-second boob flashes on Snapchat. Bet you didn't know about that, huh?'

'I don't care about anybody else. *You're* my

daughter. I want to protect you.'

I cover my face, panicking cos I've lost control of the situation. 'I can't live like this, Mum! You say one thing and then make me do the other. I feel like I'm split down the middle: one half is the real me and the other is some fake version who only exists to keep the old gossips happy. You're making me into Dad! You're making me two-faced!'

Mum winces and I immediately regret shouting.

'You're right. I admit I made mistakes with your dad, but I care about you more than I care what people on our street may or may not be thinking. You have to remember that I've had to lean on them in the past and they've always come through for us. They've lent us money without interest, stepped in at the last minute and childminded you when I had emergency shifts at the hospital. Now you've got us wrapped up in the middle of a scandal and nobody's going to care to learn the truth.'

'What about Tariq? He'll get a bad reputation too, won't he?'

'It's not the same . . .'

'Why? Cos I'm a girl? How is that fair?'

'It's not. People are always judging our community

and calling us backwards and patriarchal when the rest of the world is exactly the same. The world is full of double standards but, Salma, we can't afford to invite trouble.'

Mum drives silently, her jaw muscles clenched.

'But Mum, you know I'd never lie to you, right? You believe me about Tariq?'

She nods. 'But our neighbours won't. Life is just going to be that much harder when they turn their backs on us.'

'But why, Mum? After looking out for us, it makes no sense.'

'In their minds a line's been crossed.'

'Yeah, in their minds; not in real life. Anyway, people like Muzna won't judge us. Our generation's different than yours.'

'No?' She smiles sadly. 'Muzna's a sweet girl and Uncle Saleem and Auntie Parveen have been especially kind, but do you think they'd jeopardize their own position in the community by letting her mix with us?'

'But you didn't even do anything! And all I did was make a stupid mistake. Tariq's the one who got undressed and lied about it.' I pause for breath, seeing the worry and fatigue in every premature crease and wrinkle in Mum's face. 'I'm sorry, Mum!'

'It's my responsibility to parent you right. I'm grounding you.'

'What? You can't do that! I've got my audition in two days.'

'You just admitted that you made a mistake. I'm proud of you for that, but there have to be consequences, Salma, because that's real life.'

'But Mum!'

'It's not up for discussion. I went out of my mind looking for you. It's not what I expect after a long shift at the hospital.'

Mum drives us back in silence, while I simmer with guilt. All I wanted was to know what it would be like to date someone. *Stupid Tariq!* Somehow, in spite of all my rules and careful planning, I lost control and now everything's ruined.

No. Tariq doesn't get to spoil my acting dreams with his messed-up lies. This audition could be my big break. Whatever I have to do, whatever it takes, the show must go on.

CHAPTER 4

'It's called hair and make-up for a reason,' trills Shaista Mian – YouTube's latest MUA, repping South London in the beauty stakes. 'Hot irons make you perspire and hairsprays spit in your face. Like rude little brothers called Ilyas!' The door behind her clicks shut and she looks at the camera pointedly. 'You don't need me to tell you that sweaty and sticky does not a flawless finish make.'

Mum's at work and I'm anxiously watching Shaista's 'Get Ready With Me' vlog. Figure if I want to beat the competition, I need all the beauty hacks I can get. Defying Mum after getting grounded makes me feel sick, but I tell myself I'm doing it for the both of us.

Checking my ribbon curls in the mirror, I pull them back with a pink kitten-ear headband, and begin applying make-up under Shaista's no-nonsense guidance. I'm counting on the cerulean-blue skater dress I ordered off the internet to send subliminal messages to the casting directors, riffing off Disney's version of the fairy-tale princess. I'm not your classic blonde-haired, blue-eyed white girl but there's other stuff, important stuff, that connects us. We both lost a parent, ended up broke and bullied, and dream of a better future. For Cinderella that meant marrying the prince, for me it's about proving everybody wrong.

Finally ready, I have another wobble at the door, my stomach flipping because I'm breaking the rules. 'Gotta break a few eggs to make an omelette,' I mutter, steeling myself then heading out.

A giant magnifying glass must be floating over London today. Concentrated sunbeams scorch our city, conjuring a dancing, shimmering haze above the tarmac. Global warming I can take; global roasting, not so much.

First stop is the local Boots on the high street, where I douse myself in an *Issey Miyake* tester before being chased away by an irate assistant. A little while later, I duck inside an upmarket coffee shop, relief washing over me from the cool blast of the air-con, fluttering my flyaways and drying off my sweat. I hover by the fridge, staring longingly at the ice-cold drinks. Sadly, I'm priced out; even the water here needs a down payment. Muzna once told me there's a rare coffee that costs a bomb and is basically harvested from elephant poo. Looking at the pompous expressions of the people at the counter, that just cracks me up.

'Are you buying that?' asks a voice at my elbow, making me jump. It's a man with a trolley, looking to replenish the fridge. I glance down at the bottle in my hand sadly, then shake my head. I'm about to put it back when he speaks up.

'Take it.'

'Nah, I'm all right.'

'It's hot and you're the prettiest girl I've seen all day.' He pulls out some coin. 'I got you.'

I smile, grab the drink and beeline for the door. It's messed up that people treat you differently just cos they think you're pretty. But dehydraters can't be choosers.

Outside on the pavement I'm instantly baking again. I press the precious bottle to my forehead, rolling the cool surface over my blazing skin. There's plenty of time before I need to be at the theatre, so I meander over to the local park to brush up on my lines. I'm halfway along the winding path, admiring the clusters of brightly coloured summer flowers, before I spot trouble: a gang of boys, crowding round a kid on a bench. If there was any doubt about what's going on, the threatening laughter clinches it. *Turn around, Salma, and walk outta here alive.* Every Londoner knows not to mess with gangs unless you wanna get shanked. Plus, there's me in my boohoo glam, hardly fight wear. I'm about to duck out when I glimpse the expression on the kid's face. It's the look of a baby antelope surrounded by a pack of lions.

RUN, SALMA! RUN! screams the voice in my head, but I've never been good at taking orders, not even from myself.

'You ain't funny, fam. So piss off.' The edge in my voice is battle-honed. When you and your best mate have been bullied from a young age, you pick up survival tactics real quick or you die. Body language and tone are everything. Showing fear is asking for it.

The boys turn to look at me. Their leader — a fool in a durag and box-fresh creps — is the last one to turn around. His pit-bull snarl switches up to a smile. Every girl knows this is way worse.

'Hey, baby,' he leers. 'Where ya been all my life?'

'Given I'm sixteen, probably in school.' The sarcasm flies off me like projectile vomit.

'Well you ain't dressed for no school. You dressed for *fun*.' He makes a salacious noise, like he's just sampled steak and found it juicy.

'Actually, I'm dressed for an audition. FYI, I just got excluded for bashing some boy's brains in. Now, you gonna disappear or you gonna test me?' I'm low-key terrified, wishing a cop would walk past. Fat chance with government cuts and my luck.

'Ooooh!' cry his mates, lapping it up.

'Oil-wrestle it out!' suggests another, cracking his mates up.

'Nah, baby girl . . .' the leader coos, walking round me like he's sizing up the goods. His voice drops to a horribly intimate whisper, brushing curls away from my right ear. 'King don't want to upset his queen.'

'Then you'd best get home to her, innit? Pretty sure she'd be mad jealous seeing you now.'

His warm breath tickles my ear. '*You* wanna see what I got?'

'Nah, I'm all right. So how about you leave me and my boyfriend the hell alone?'

The entire gang's eyes pop out like they got told

the world's about to end in five. Even the victim looks like he swallowed a golf ball.

'Y-your *boyfriend*?' he stammers, blinking. 'Nah, you ain't dating this queer.'

I clutch the kid's sweaty hand. 'Bruh, we're Haringey's most loved-up; practically married. Ya don't believe me? Check out our Insta stories.' The poor kid finally gets it, slipping an arm around my shoulders.

'Yeah,' he agrees in a nervous squeak. 'Me and . . . er . . . Jasmine were voted cutest couple.'

Jasmine? It takes every bit of my self-control to pull the breaks on an eye-roll.

'On Valentine's Day,' I add. Hoping to plaster over the cracks of our fragile lies. Because the other option is violence and in spite of all the self-defence classes Mum got me I doubt I can take a gang of six teenage boys. Least of all their leader who looks like he's pushing six foot.

'Nah, man,' says one of the boys, getting riled up, his body language exaggerated and choppy. 'This girl be disrespecting you.'

'Shut up!' snaps the leader. 'Princess Jasmine here has asked us to go and that's exactly what we're

gonna do . . . right after she gives me her number.'
He pushes an iPhone Pro Max into my trembling
hand, pressing his sweaty skin to mine.

'Forget it,' I say. 'I don't know you.'

'Where my manners at?' He pulls the durag off
his head and bows. For one moment, I stare at his
cornrows – each one as flawless as a string of black
pearls. Don't think I've ever seen an Asian guy with
hair like that before. 'I'm Imran.' He dimples and
adds with a knowing wink, 'But you get to call me
"boo" or *mera ishq*, innit? All ya gotta do is gimme
one missed call, baby girl, and I can make dis all go
away.' He spreads his arms, gesturing to his feral
squad.

Normally, when a boy asks for my number I
fob him off with a fake, but faking a missed call is
impossible. This one's sly. Reluctantly I pull my
phone out, dreading turning it on in case Mum's left
a ton of messages. The phone screen lights up but
there are zero messages. *Oof.* Imran calls his number
out as I type it in then press the green phone icon. A
ringtone like Beenie Man or Alkaline fills the park.

'Aye!' he says, making his phone vanish. 'Good
luck with your audition, Princess Jasmine. Give

man a call later, yeah?' He points at the kid, 'I know you guys ain't dating but take care of her anyway. A'ight?'

The kid nods obediently.

'And,' Imran pauses, suddenly less sure of himself. 'Sorry about that stuff I said earlier, yeah? Was having a laugh, mate. We cool?'

'Totally,' he replies.

When the crew are a safe distance away, and quite definitely not coming back, I deflate.

'Thanks! I owe you my life,' gushes the kid. 'God, I wish I was as pretty as you.'

Looking up in surprise, I notice for the first time that he's wearing lipstick, clumpy mascara and cakey foundation, in a shade that would even look fake on an orange.

'And now you can see why they were bullying me.'

'N-no,' I say, ashamed of wearing my thoughts on my sleeve. 'You caught me off guard, is all. I thought—'

'See, that's the thing about cis-folk: always making assumptions.' He frames the words with finger quotes like he's scratching out somebody's eyes.

'Well what are you?' I ask.

'I'm Billie. At least I will be once I can legally change my name.'

'So . . . you're a girl?' I suggest, trying to keep up.

'No. My pronouns are they/them. I'm enby.'

'OK!' I say brightly, knowing I sound fake.

'Don't worry, nobody ever gets it.'

I press my skirt against my legs, sitting on the bench. 'Hey, just cos someone doesn't get you, don't mean they don't want to.'

Billie studies me, as if trying to work out whether I'm taking the piss. 'Sorry, I'm so tired of being seen as a joke. There's even some people in the LGBT community who give me grief.'

'Yeah, well, I know a little something about communities judging you even though they've had to deal with judgemental crap too.' I stare at a couple of bedraggled pigeons fighting over a chicken wing. Birds eating bird – I swear London is getting crazier every day.

'The difference is you've got pretty privilege. The world's a lot more accepting when you're getting called Princess Jasmine by a hot thug.'

'Yeah, well, pretty ain't everything.' I hug myself,

feeling small and vulnerable.

'Oh boohoo!' Billie snaps making me jump. 'Being a hot girl must be such a drag. I mean look at those poor Kardashian-Jenners and every bikini babe on every reality TV show ever. Getting paid millions to pout must be so *traumatizing*!' That escalated quickly.

'That's not my life . . .' I mutter.

'No? You just got a gang of alphas to back down. Think you could've pulled off that minor miracle if you weren't so hot?'

I turn to face them. 'I'm poor, brown and my community think I'm a skank. Still wanna trade places? I got excluded for two weeks and I'm disobeying my mum to go to this audition. You jealous, fam? All of y'all get to have an opinion about a "hot girl" – everybody but *herself*.' The pigeons coo in alarm and take flight. 'What – I have to be friends with the mean girls just cos I look a certain way? Hell to the no! My best mate is this girl with literally tons of talent but people are always asking why I'm friends with *her*, like I owe them an explanation for their own dumb prejudices. I got guys like that Imran hitting on me when all I want is to be left alone. And when I won't put out, I get called a ho and suddenly everybody's hating on me. Like how does that even make sense?'

'OK, OK! I hear you!' Billie says making me realize I'm ranting. '*Jeez*!'

'You know something?' I say, glaring at Billie. 'You can shut up anyway cos you're pretty too.' Billie gives me an eye-roll. 'You are but—'

Billie's eyes cut sharply back to me, defensive and vulnerable. 'But what?'

'You're crap at doing make-up.'

Their lips form a bright red 'O'.

'C'mere,' I say, rifling through my bag. 'Auntie Salma'll give you a makeover.'

'Salma? I thought it was Jasmine.'

'Nope, *you* made that up.'

Billie blushes. 'I guess everyone's a little guilty of making assumptions.'

I scrub a make-up wipe over Billie's delicate features, a legal requirement before attempting any sort of glow up.

'OK.' I give Billie winged eyeliner, smoke it out with my eyeshadow pallet, then apply a bold aquamarine pigment to the corner of their eyes.

Billie folds their arms, frowning. 'I hate school. People think being non-binary is a fad. I get called a "shim" or "Ladyboy Gaga". Then there's some idiots who tell me they identify as a unicorn or a dragon. Like what the actual frick?'

I shake my head and sigh. Poor Billie trusting me with all this private info. Guess offloading to a complete stranger is low stakes. 'I feel you. But hey, my . . .' I check myself, not wanting to mention Mum for some reason. 'Someone told me there's like a tribe of people in Pakistan called *khusre*. They're legally recognized as the third sex and they've been around forever.'

'I didn't know that about Pakistan.'

'Why would you? With the amount of hate going on in the media, it's hardly surprising.' I screw the lid back on the lip gloss and admire my handiwork. Holding my phone out I ask: 'What do you think?'

Billie's delight is so obvious it's cute.

'Hashtag no filter,' I add.

Billie tears up. 'You made me look pretty! I always wanted to know what this feels like. You're like Queer Eye and my fairy godmother in one.'

'Actually . . . it's *Cinderella* I'm aiming for,'

I explain. 'That's the role I'm up for.'

'Sick! I hope whoever's doing the casting isn't sold on Cinders being a white girl.'

'That, my enby friend, is exactly what I'm counting on. Cinderella's race has zero to do with the actual story.'

Billie smiles. 'You're *way* prettier than Disney's version. Plus you can kick some actual man-arse.'

'Thanks.' I furrow my brow. 'Man-arse, woman-arse, non-gender-specific-arse: don't let the glass slippers fool you. If a butt needs kicking, I'm on it.'

Billie chuckles.

'So you bunking cos of the bullying?' I ask.

'What time's your audition?' Billie counters, avoiding my question.

'Any time between nine and four.'

'Great. That's more than enough time for me to buy you an ice cream. It's the least I can do for making me look gorge.'

We walk past the hissing fountains and towards the large iron gates, shadow and sunlight dappling our path like marble.

Parked a little way up the road is an OG ice-cream van. The 'Teddy Bears' Picnic' floats towards us on a cushion of warm air like reheated memories from a time when life wasn't such a struggle. Back when Muzna and me could be friends without families and communities and boys having a say in it. Every inch of the van's windows are plastered in stickers advertising the delicious and the divine. A queue of mostly office staff snakes round the side of the van, wilting under the intense heat yet desperate for the fleeting release of a frozen dessert. A tinny voice on somebody's tablet is ranting about it being the hottest day of the year.

'Tell us something we don't know,' mutters a lady, fanning herself with an envelope, earning some laughs.

'This isn't all for me!' says another woman defensively, carrying a cardboard tray of four sundaes back to her office.

Seven years ago, Mum took me and Muzna to see a musical version of *Rumpelstiltskin* at the local theatre. I was mesmerized. The costumes, the singing, the dancing and, of course, the acting was on point and sent my eight-year-old brain into a frenzy. Guess you could say it was the moment the acting bug got its fangs in me. To possess the power to make people laugh, fall in love and cry was mind-blowing. For the entire time you were up on stage, creating magic, you were living somebody else's life. It meant I wouldn't have to think about Dad, or how hard Mum worked, or how difficult school was.

Billie thrusts an ice lolly into my clenched fist. 'Wow, you looked super mad.'

'Wha?' Feeling exposed, I cover with a snicker. 'Million miles away.'

'Yeah?' Billie says licking fluorescent-pink bubblegum sauce off the top of their ice cream. A sugar unicorn horn pokes out of the side, coloured like a pastel rainbow. 'So what's a nice girl like you getting excluded for?'

I sink my teeth through the delicious orange ice shell of my lolly, tasting vanilla ice cream and fruit sorbet beneath. 'I think the more important question is: why do you bunk when kids bully you? Why not report it to a teacher or your parents?'

A rose glow spreads over Billie's cheeks which has nothing to do with the blush I applied earlier. 'I skip school every now and then when things get too intense. I'm sick of having to explain myself. Why can't teachers just protect me for being me?'

'They don't do jack?'

'They do, but it always comes with *advice.*' Billie's fingers dance like flashing quotes. ' "*If you stop wearing make-up to school and dying your hair bright colours, people will probably leave you alone.*" '

'Victim-blaming,' I say, scowling. 'Yesterday I got slut-shamed and complained to the Head. Says she'll look into it but reckons it wouldn't happen if I didn't dress *inappropriately.* And I'm the one who gets excluded.'

'Jeez!' Billie trills, nearly dropping their ice cream. 'They're all the same. And I'm literally being told to stop being *me.*'

'But you can do you when you're older and no longer *their* problem?'

'Exactly! See, you get it.' Billie licks the pink sauce off their fingers. 'I get super stressy and can't concentrate in school unless I feel like me. I've given up correcting people for using wrong pronouns. I should at least be allowed to exist in peace.' I place a hand on Billie's shoulder and give it a squeeze. 'Wish my stupid mother let me be home-schooled! She's like, "Everyone gets bullied at high school, it's a rite of passage." Blah, blah, blah and

I should "Stop being a baby".'

Hearing Billy diss his mum like that makes me think of my own. Mum grounded me for getting in a mess with Tariq but at least she believed I was innocent.

'Did you tell your mum what the bullying's about, though?'

'You practically told Imran you bashed a boy's brains in. C'mon, I need details!' Billie asks clapping their hands, once again dodging my question.

Really not wanting to revisit it, I give them the CliffNotes version. 'We went on a date together and I fell asleep. Y'know? Too much fried chicken. Then he takes this posed picture making it look like stuff happened between us on a first date. The picture gets shared around and pretty soon I'm the biggest ho in town.'

Billie swears and covers their mouth. 'Sorry but that's dumpster-tier nasty! Then what happened?'

I cover my face, rubbing my eyes. 'I confronted him, demanding a public apology. Then he starts telling everyone about my audition, made me look like some foolish child. You do not do that, fam! That's personal; that's somebody's dreams. So I went crazy and tried to beat him up. Next thing I know, I'm being dragged to the Head's office.'

'Yaas, queen!' Billie says clapping. 'Smash the patriarchy!'

'This is real life, Billie, where nobody's crowning queens or attacking the patriarchy.' I squeeze my fists together. 'Boy got me so mad, it's like I split into two people. The one beating him up – the one in control of my body – just didn't care. *She did not care.* The rest of me was as shocked as everybody else.'

'You don't seem like the sort of girl who goes around attacking people.'

'Ya think? Sometimes I feel like I'm going crazy, pretending to be two different people, keeping up appearances and that. All I want is to be the real me. Why is that such a big deal?'

'Hell if I know,' Billie says crossly. 'Maybe you're just too special for this world?'

'And if I'm mental?'

'Finish your Solero and let's go to this audition of yours,' Billie says, stemming my self-doubts.

'You coming?'

'Miss out on my new bestie getting Cinderella? Wouldn't miss it for the world.'

I mirror their smile then falter when my phone starts ringing. I place it on the bench between us, glancing at the number on the screen. 'It's Mum.'

Billie pulls out their own phone and checks the time. 'You gonna answer it?'

I shake my head with fear.

'Your mum, she's not supportive then?'

'I know my dad would've taken a running jump at the River Thames rather than have an actor for a daughter. Mum . . . not gonna lie: she lets me do stuff. She lets me wear what I want, even if it does upset some of the aunties. But she's mad that I ended up in the middle of a big sexy scandal, so I'm grounded.'

'I honestly think you should just explain to her how much this opportunity means to you. Give her a chance, eh?'

'It's not that simple. Everyone thinks wanting to be an actor is a bimbo's dream. That winning a part is like the lottery: it could happen to literally anyone but the odds are stacked against you. I have to prove to Mum that I can get this part, not cos of what I look like or dumb luck, but cos of what I can do. That I'm talented enough to make a career out of it,' I say firmly.

CHAPTER 5

We walk up the high street, towards the bus stop.

'You said most actors are out of work,' Billie says. 'So why do you even want to do it then?'

'Because I can't help it.' I search for better words but come up short. 'In spite of all the backlash I might get, the lack of money, the online trolling, I just know I need to do it. Acting makes me feel *alive*. I definitely don't want to do sensible. Mum spent her whole life doing that and it made her miserable. But she does it anyway cos she's got a kid and Dad's debts to pay off.

'I want to be the girl who takes risks and owns her life. Not the girl who dies wondering if things could've turned out differently, y'know?'

'I wish I could be as brave as you . . .' Billie says looking away. 'You asked me earlier why my mum hasn't helped me with the bullies. It's because I haven't told her. I mean, I tried back when I thought I might be gay and she went ballistic. She started quoting the Bible at me and said she wouldn't speak to me again until I apologized.'

'Apologize for being gay?' I ask in disbelief.

Billie nods. 'Every day I leave home looking like a boy. I pop into the loos at McDonald's, spray my hair and put on my make-up. Then I go to school and get bullied. I have to wash it all off before I go home again.'

'I'm sorry,' I say.

We walk in mutual silence, worrying about letting down the people we love.

'You said the play is a modern take on Cinderella. What's modern about it?' Billie asks trying to brighten the mood.

I brush a spiral curl behind my ear. 'To be honest there's not that much info on their website. It's definitely legit though cos Edwina Hirsch is an absolute legend and she's the prime judge. What I do know is it's set in high school. No magic, no helpful animals. Cinderella has to think her way out of a bad situation. The quirky nerds like her, but the popular kids don't. Oh, and the prince isn't royal either. He's just some dude called Prinz who ends up becoming prom king . . . and I'm guessing he asks Cinderella to be his prom queen?'

Billie claps their hands together. 'Promise me!'

'What?'

'That if you get this role, I get a free ticket on opening night! It sounds sick.'

We board the bus, pressing Zip cards to the electronic reader and tripping down the aisle. Spotting a couple of seats in the middle, we crash down on them. I notice a blue sign asking us to give them up if an old person, a pregnant woman or person carrying a baby is in need. I make a mental note to do that.

'Salma, *beyti*?'

I stiffen recognizing that awful husky voice. Glancing back, the horror becomes real when I see Auntie Balquis and her bougie shopping bags spread across two seats, a hideous smile plastered on her plum-painted lips. Stubby fingers coil over the rail, displaying eight gleaming rings like twenty-four-carat-gold knuckle dusters. I cower from the most powerful and gossipy of all the aunties in my neighbourhood. The two houses next door to us belong to her extended family, fused into one great big palace of gossip, drama and extravaganza.

'*Asalaamu alaykum*, Auntie-*ji*,' I say meekly.

'Where are you two girls going in the middle of a school day?'

I consider hitting the emergency door release and booking it. 'Er, work experience.'

'Dressed like this?' She rotates her hands and thrusts them at me in despair. 'You look like you're going to a party. That dress is far too tight and I can see your shameless legs.'

'There's nothing shameless about her legs!' Billie snaps. 'She's beautiful.'

Auntie's pencilled eyebrows shoot to the black roots of her honey-brown dyed hair. '*Hai, hai!* It's a boy in make-up. Is this transvestite bothering you?'

Billie flushes.

'Billie's my friend,' I say in weak defiance, my insides shrivelling.

Rudely switching to Urdu in company, she says 'What sort of friend is this? You must be very careful around such people.'

I reply in Urdu. 'So just cos my friend is wearing a bit of make-up you think they're dangerous? You know what you are? A bloody hypocrite!'

'And what is that supposed to mean?'

I turn away, biting back my reply. Everyone knows not to mess with Auntie Balquis – she's like a feminist fantasy gone wrong. She switches back to

English. 'Anyway, where are you going and don't lie to me about work experience.'

'She's going to an audition for Cinderella and she's going to nail it!' Billie says proudly.

I glower at Billie but it's too late. The cat's out of the bag.

'Audition? You want to become an actress? *A kanjari*? Your father must be spinning in his grave!' She pulls her phone out of an oxblood leather handbag the size of a small suitcase. 'I'm going to tell your mother.'

Panic sets in. 'She works in A&E. Don't you think she has bigger things to worry about?'

'Bigger than the honour of her daughter?' Her kohl-encircled eyes give me a chastising glare.

'Are you OK?' Billie asks, noticing me welling up.

I wipe a tear away. 'I wanna get off this bus.'

'Come on, let's go.'

Heading for the doors, my dress gets caught on an old woman's knitting needle. 'Mind out!' she snaps, attacking my dress with violence. I yank myself free of her knitting, stumbling off the bus.

Auntie Balquis shakes her head. 'Poor Tariq being misled by a harlot. Your father's curse on you!'

'I don't get it,' Billie says out on the pavement. 'All day I've watched you be nothing but fierce. Now you let that opinionated cow walk all over you?'

'You don't understand.'

'Why, because I'm white?'

I'm done. 'Actually yeah. Everybody in my community looks up to Auntie Balquis. She's like the matriarch or something. Nobody crosses her. Ever.'

'Well call me an insensitive white person but she was flat-out bullying you. Why would anyone look up to a witch like her?'

'She's rich. Most of us have been on hard times at some point in our lives and she's been there to lend money. Interest free.' I frown, clutching my forehead. 'Only it's not. The price is your soul. Mum borrowed cash to pay off some of Dad's loans. We still owe her.'

Billie folds their arms tightly. 'Lending money doesn't give someone the right to look down on people or control their lives.'

'See? Told you, you wouldn't understand.'

I walk off, leaving Billie looking hurt.

CHAPTER 6

Billie chases me down the street, calling out, but I'm so mad-frustrated I can't seem to stop. My head is filled with Auntie Balquis grassing me up to Mum. I can't. Not when I'm this close to achieving my dream.

'Please!' Billie cries out. 'I'm sorry. What more can I say? It's too hot to be fighting and you're sweating out your lovely dress.'

They're right. My armpits are freaking Jacuzzis.

Billie manages to coax me back to the bus stop. There are a couple of red-faced women waiting under the shelter; one with a lace fan and the other using a glossy magazine to deflect the sun. It's so hot, I swear my sweat is sizzling. Pulling out a tissue, I pat my face, freaking out at the pink-brown-black mess smeared on it.

'Don't worry,' Billie says. 'We can fix it when we get to the theatre.'

'Forget it, hun. Even James Charles, Huda Kattan and Shaista Mian put together couldn't fix this mess. Only one thing for it.' I blitz my face with a make-up wipe, enjoying the cooling sensation of cucumber and aloe.

'You're going nude?' Billie shrieks, making the two women glare at us.

'Could you say that a bit louder, please? I think some pervy dudes on the opposite side missed it.'

'Sorry, I just . . . I think I would have the mother of all panic attacks without my warpaint, even though I don't have half your skills.'

'It's just pigment and fat,' I say with a shrug. 'An actor – a real actor – doesn't need props. She creates in the imagination.'

We both crack up. After the horror of Auntie Balquis, it's just what the doctor ordered.

A jogger with a shaved head and black running shorts pauses, plucking out an ear bud. 'There's been an incident on London Bridge,' he says gesturing in the direction he's come from. 'It's affecting buses and transport.'

'Oh, for the love of . . .' snaps one woman, dropping her magazine.

'Pathetic!' snipes the other, giving a flamenco crack of her fan. 'It's all that ruddy mayor's fault. Never used to be this bad before he arrived. Thank heavens for Uber.'

'Hey, thanks, yeah?' I say to the jogger for saving us an endless wait in the sweltering heat.

He nods, gives a brief smile, then jogs on.

'OMG that guy was flipping hot!' Billie whispers breathlessly, fanning themselves.

Suddenly the world is closing in all around me, I'm struggling to breathe and I see no way out of the mess I'm in. 'OK, I'm done.' I cuss, not caring about the disapproving look I get from the lady waiting for her taxi.

'Salma, we've still got three hours. Hopefully the buses'll be running again soon.' Suddenly, Billie gasps, placing their hand on their chest. I follow Billie's eyes to the hemline of my dress.

'Oh my life!' I shriek, gaping at the massive tear in the skirt. 'This cannot be happening. It was my wear-and-return dress.'

'Calm down.'

'I've had a knitting-needle-related wardrobe fail and you're telling me to calm down? That old hag musta been knitting with knives!'

'Relax, I saw a Fabulous Farah back there.' Billie jerks their thumb over their shoulder.

'You tripping? I don't have cash to splash. I'mma

have to buy safety pins and make do.' Even as I say it, I realize fixing this mess is impossible. Forget cats, my dress looks like it was mauled by a tiger.

'Look, this has seriously been one of the best days of my life. I'm Billie-one-mate. People like me don't usually get to hang out with people like you.'

'Like me?'

'You're beautiful and talented and you can defeat a gang of thugs without lifting a finger. You're goddess tier. Me? I'm just an embarrassment to my mum.'

A large black Ford Galaxy collects the women who I guess have decided to share the fare.

'You're not an embarrassment to nobody,' I say in solidarity.

'Mum thinks God made men to be men and women to be women. She caught me trying on one of her dresses once and said if I ever did it again she'd put me in care.'

'You serious? Who says that to their kids?' I catch myself. Sometimes Dad said worse and I know a lot of people in my community would be exactly the same.

'I tried to stop,' Billie continues. 'I don't say I'm non-binary for the attention – I'd be so much happier if people didn't notice me because most of the time when they do, they just look at me like I'm a freak.'

I put an arm around Billie. 'Not gonna lie: I don't completely get it but you're definitely not doing it for the attention.'

Billie's brow forms a map of worry lines, desperate for me to understand their truth. 'Look, just like you *knew* you were a girl when you were little, that's when I *knew* I wasn't a boy or a girl. It literally has nothing to do with sexuality.'

'Wasn't that scary?'

'Why would it be? I was too young to realize enbys got hate just for being.'

'That gets me so mad, cos you're such a nice person! Like how does being non-binary affect anyone else anyway?'

Billie looks down at their hands, fingers knotted together. 'It affects my mum. She gave me life.'

'So? You ain't some toy out of a Kinder Surprise she gets to play swapsies with. You're the only person who gets to decide who you are. And a good mum would love you for it.' My eyes drift to the sky, remembering a conversation I had with Mum last year. It was the moment I told her I was dead serious about being an actor.

'If it's what you want to do, I'll support you,' Mum had said, looking worried. 'But you need to know it's not going to be easy. Put yourself up on a stage and you're giving everyone an opportunity to judge you. People can be cruel. Casting directors, reviewers, jealous actors, award judges and the audience – they'll all have an opinion. Not to mention there are people in our community who think acting is un-Islamic. But if it's what you really want, I'll back you up. I just need for you to be prepared.'

My encounter with Auntie Balquis brought all this home. But I reckon there'll be supporters as well as haters, people who've waited their whole lives for someone from the community to represent them. 'Know what, B? We need to quit apologizing for being fricking fabulous.'

Billie starts to laugh. 'Come on, Cinders! At this rate, it'll be flipping midnight before you get to your audition. We're going to Fabulous Farah and that's that. I've got a credit card.'

A credit card: the magic wand that's been missing my whole life.

Billie hustles me to the department store. After this crazy day and all the hoops I've had to jump through, I'm surprised that I still want to go. I realize I want this gig more than anything I've ever wanted in my whole life.

Fabulous Farah's is the kind of shop I avoid unless there's a massive sale on. Slate-grey mannequins with giant velvet flowers for heads stare blankly out of shop displays giving nightmarish vibes of Wonderland. At least Alice's bitchy flowers had roots. I keep checking over my shoulder to make sure these monsters haven't shifted from their pedestals.

The place is packed with high-class tourists, turning their noses up at everything. Billie grabs my hand and guides me over to a rack of evening dresses. 'This is pretty.'

I look at the slinky black velvet number they're stroking as if it were a pet. I pull a face. 'I'm up for Cinderella, remember? Not Maleficent.'

'I like Maleficent,' Billie says as I move past the bodycons and maxis towards the skater dresses.

'You an Angelina fan, huh?'

'No, I like the cartoon one. She was boobless, taller than the men, and with a face that was harsher than your typical girl's face. I related to her.'

I laugh. 'You saying she was OG enby? Oh, look!' I say, swiping a baby-blue dress off the clothes rack and holding it against me.

'Way better than the one you're wearing.' Billie says then adds in a falsetto voice, 'You shall go to the ball and you're going to be lit.'

I check my watch, making sure there's enough time, then grab the dress they were stroking. 'Let's go try them on.'

Billie stops stock still, causing me to knock into them. 'We can't! I mean *I* can't. They'll never let me—' I place a finger over their lips.

I yank Billie along, fixing the shop assistant gatekeeping the changing rooms with a winning smile. 'We're trying on two dresses, thanks.'

The assistant's eyes shift to Billie who is doing an impression of a beetroot.

'You got a problem?' I ask the assistant pointedly, sliding out my phone. 'We're shopaholic influencers. We'll be reviewing our experience later to our ten thousand followers.'

'Oh, I see,' says the assistant looking rather flustered. She fiddles behind her counter and hands us tokens. I grab Billie and drag them to the changing cubicles.

'I'm not supposed to be here!' Billie says miserably, speaking in barely more than a whisper.

'Nobody cares, B. Separate cubicles with separate curtains. Could anything be more private? Plus, I'll be next door.' Billie looks uncertain so I make a hand puppet out of the black dress, manipulating black velvet lips in sync with my words. 'I'm so soft and just dying to be worn. Together we could place evil curses on spinning wheels and rule the world! Mwahahaha!'

Billie covers their face and giggles. 'I've never done this before.'

Inside my cubicle, I pull on the dress, feeling the fabric whisper over my skin. Glancing in the mirror, I see a silhouette that makes me break out in a smile. Somehow the delicate blue makes my brown skin glow (though that might just be the diffused lighting).

'Oh. My. God.'

My ears perk up and I hastily knock on the thin cubicle wall. 'You all right, hun?'

'They use fake mirrors in changing rooms, don't they?' Billie's voice is tender and frail.

'What, like hall of mirrors? That what you mean?'

'Yeah, warping the glass to make you look good. I think that's what they've got in here,' Billie says with a heavy sigh.

'You need a second opinion. Budge up, cos here it comes!' Billie starts to protest, as I knew they would, but I thrust myself behind the curtain anyway.

'Fam . . .' I say, startled.

'I look stupid, don't I? I'll take it off . . .' Billie drops their eyes, undoing the zipper.

'Don't you dare!' I say, slapping the hand away. 'You got the drip, B.' I watch their face light up. 'You look good cos you feel good. And you're feeling good cos you're expressing whatever fabulousness is hiding inside. Amirite?'

Billie nods, unable to take their eyes of their reflection in case it's as fleeting as a puff of smoke. 'Omigosh!' Billie says, placing a hand on their chest. 'You look *incredible*.'

'Two pretty people and a mobile phone? Must be TikTok o'clock!'

Calling up the app on my phone, I record us lip syncing to *Don't Cha*, struggling to keep straight faces. I lose it when Billie starts voguing.

'Don't think I've ever had this much fun!' Billie says, fanning themselves. 'OK, let's buy your dress and get out of here before somebody reports us.'

My smile falters as reality sets in. 'I'm afraid to look at the price tag . . .'

'My mum's paying so who cares?' Billie giggles then flips the tag. 'Sixty. No problem.'

'Are you sure?' Even though it feels a lot longer, I've only known them a hot minute. Dipping into Billie's bank of mum seems wrong.

'Positive. Now give me some space so I can switch back into my civvies. But you keep that dress on. We won't have time for you to change again.'

'B, buy the black dress. You know you want to,' I say, sliding out of their cubicle.

'Nah,' Billie says sadly. 'One dress I could explain away as a gift for "my girlfriend". Two and Mum'd arrange for Reverend Johnson to come round and perform an exorcism.'

It breaks my heart. Poor Billie just wants to be themself and the person closest to them keeps judging them for something that's not even their fault. In a way, Billie reminds me of Muzna. I find that I no longer feel betrayed or hate her for giving me the silent treatment. Her note said her parents were forcing her. Mum's never done that to me. We discuss things and maybe she gets the last word but at least she always listens to what I have to say.

I take my phone out, wondering whether I should give her a call and fess up about going to the audition she banned me from. I discover I'm too chicken.

Billie guides me over to the counter. 'Can you ring it up while she's wearing it, sort of thing? We're late.'

The sales girl looks flustered than asks me to turn around so she can scan the barcode and remove the tag.

'It might take me a year or two, but I'mma pay you back, B,' I swear.

Billie hushes me, taking out a platinum credit card and promptly drops it twice.

'You all right?' I ask.

They nod but I can't help noticing a sweaty sheen has formed over their upper lip and they keep blinking like a clockwork doll. The lady places my ripped dress in a bag and we walk out.

HONK! HONK! HONK!

The store alarms go off, security scanners lighting

up like the emergency services in traffic. I nearly jump out of my skin as a large security guard saunters over.

'Nothing to worry about!' Billie says waving at him. 'The lady at the till forgot to deactivate the tag is all.' What the heck is Billie chatting about? She *did* deactivate it.

'Come back in, please,' the guard says in an intimidating baritone.

I'm about to do just that when Billie yanks my arm. 'RUN!' And with that, they make a mad dash out of the automatic doors. I'm frozen in bewilderment, trying to figure out what's going on.

'Oi!' roars the security guard. One look at his furious face, his outstretched hand and I run for my life.

Billie's waves to me from the top of the escalators, before shoving people aside as they scuttle down.

'B!' I call after them, slipping through the shoppers like butter through a knife. 'What the hell? You paid for my dress, right? Let's go back and clear this up.'

'Can't!' Billie squeaks. 'I stole the black one. I didn't mean to. I just . . . I couldn't buy it and I couldn't say goodbye either.'

'Oh, Billie!' I glance behind and see the wide-shouldered security guard struggling to get through the shoppers thronging on the escalators.

'Make for the toyshop over there!' Billie says gesturing with a flick of their chin then sprints off.

'What have you got me into?' I cry. Threading through the tourists, my heels hammer the floor like mini pickaxes as I run. The security guard barrels after us. Elbowing a path for myself, I make it to the toyshop but Billie is nowhere to be seen. A yelp has me spinning round. The security guard is clutching Billie by the scruff of their neck, yelling at them. I bite my lip, shrinking back into the crowd. I could make tracks, save myself, get to the audition on time: after all *I* didn't steal anything.

But just as I couldn't leave Billie to the mercy of Imran's gang, I can't leave them now.

'Hey, wait up!' I call as the security guard is frogmarching Billie back to Fabulous Farah's.

We sit together on one side of a table in a room that is so nondescript it's a couple of cushions short of a padded cell. Sunlight floods through the blinds behind us, charring our necks. On the other side of the table, shunning the chair, stands the security guard, spreading his hands wide, glowering at us. Billie is snivelling, all smudged lipstick and running mascara. I've learned never to show my feelings, but on the inside I am shook.

'Clever!' barks the security guard. 'Pay for one dress, steal another.'

'No one was teefing nothing,' I explain. 'My friend forgot to put the other dress back is all. Easy mistake, innit?'

'What? Stuffed it in his backpack and zipped it up by mistake?' The sarcasm is real. 'You know, I could call the police and have you both arrested.'

Billie gasps, wringing their hands together.

'But you wouldn't do that, would you?' I suggest, giving my prettiest smile. 'You seem like a nice guy who wouldn't wanna spoil a coupla teenagers' lives. Specially when they owned up that they made a dumb mistake and they are so, so sorry.'

The guard taps his lips thoughtfully then places a pad down in front of us. 'Pick up that pen. I want your full names and your parents' numbers. And no funny business!'

'Oh, please don't!' Billie begs. 'My mum is literally worse than the police.'

The guard cocks an eyebrow. 'So you'd rather I call the cops then?'

I shake my head. 'No, we wouldn't.' I scribble on the pad. 'There. That's both our names and numbers. We are sorry, you know?'

He snorts, turning the pad his way, looking from one to the other, flexing his jaw muscles. 'Wait here.'

The moment the door clicks, I grab Billie, yanking them to their feet. 'Help me get this window open!'

Billie doesn't need to be told twice. Shoving aside the blinds, we turn the handles and push it open. Practically falling over one another, we leap out of the window and make a bolt for freedom.

'We're free!' Billie shouts as we exit the alleyway, running along the back of the building and across the road. 'Squeeeeeeee!'

'Hold that squeee 'til we're on the bus!'

Two minutes later, we're safely hidden at the back of the bus and the driver is en route to the Fortuna Theatre. 'Honestly, B, what the hell were you thinking? In what world is stealing a dress not a crime?'

Billie covers their face in shame. 'I was more afraid of coming out to my mum as non-binary than getting a criminal record for stealing. How messed-up is that? I guess I just wanted to do something crazy to prove I can make decisions. But I'm sorry I got you into trouble.'

My frown thaws. 'Guess you ain't had it easy, hun. It's not for me to tell you to come out. But I'll tell you this for free: Auntie Balquis is gonna blab to everyone on my street that I'm going to be an actress. She'll get it twisted, make it sound dirty and link it to the fake selfie my fake boyfriend took of some faked-up stuff that never happened. But once it's out there, I don't have to care any more. I'll be free!'

'But suppose you get excommunicated by your community?'

The bus jerks to a stop.

'Then I'll just have to find my own way. The world is big enough for everyone, B. Worrying about stuff is the worst. That's the thing that kills you.'

Billie considers this then hugs me. 'You're right. Thanks, hun. Craziest day ever?'

'Amen!'

'Everyone off the bus!' the driver calls, making

my heart stop. 'I've called an engineer for repairs, but it's gonna take a while for him to get here.'

Outside, on the pavement, I'm wondering why everything keeps going wrong. Auntie Balquis said Dad would curse me from beyond the grave for shaming our family. As stupid as that sounds, could that be what this is?

'I don't have lizards for footmen,' Billie says, taking out their phone, 'mice for white horses, or even a pumpkin for a coach, but I'm maxing out my credit card and calling you an Uber.'

CHAPTER 7

The odds were stacked like a mountain, God only knows how many rules we broke, and we cut it so fine that the guy at the desk refused to register us. Begging and pleading wasn't working either. If it hadn't been for three more girls turning up after us and arguing up a storm, I'd be sitting on the steps outside the Fortuna Theatre right now, crying my eyes out.

Instead, I'm standing at the back of a queue of preening girls and prickly stage mums. They're sizing each other up, evaluating their chances. Seems like every last one of them is perfectly turned out and immaculately dressed. Then I spot a girl biting her nails, looking up at her mother every couple of minutes like she's a prison officer. I smile at her. Her smile is brief and sad, like she'd rather be anywhere but here. I can kind of relate. Five minutes in the toilets was barely enough time to sort my scraggly hair or blot my oily skin. The dress is fabulous but the girl inside is trash. Suddenly I'm yearning for Mum so bad, I think I'm going to cry.

'Will you stop doing that to yourself?!' Billie chides as the last three girls join the back of the queue.

'You lost me.'

'Worrying. Look, you know your lines, your improv piece is brilliant, your face was made for close-ups and you said you wanted to be an actor more than anything in the entire history of wanting things. And we made it in time!'

'It's not that simple. These girls are quality, you can see it in the way they stand. They've had years of training and they probably have friends in high places. Why am I putting myself through this, B? Not only do I have to outshine all this talent, but I have to make the casting directors think outside the box too.'

'I feel your pain,' Billie confides. 'I didn't tell you this before. In primary, I wanted to play Dorothy so bad in the school play but got shot down for being "a boy".' The finger quotes Billie is so fond of are out again with a vengeance. 'I was a coward. I am a coward. You're not like me, Salma. You're a fierce queen.'

I shake my head. 'Next to this lot, I'm like

something that got stuck to a glass slipper.'

'Really? Show me one other girl who went through hell and high water to be here. You don't need a stage mother to do the talking, like these other girls do. Your talent will speak volumes. Go out there, Salma; go before those judges and whatever prejudices they're holding on to, and send the other girls sashaying away.' Billie snaps their fingers. 'Because you were born for this. Shantay, you stay.'

'You're making me cry!' I hug Billie.

'Oh my God, they're so fake!' whispers one hopeful but I take it in my stride. She may look like classic Cinderella, but she has the heart of an ugly sister. The glass slipper can only fit one of us, but even if it's not me it won't mean I have to give up my acting dreams. Hollywood's full of stories about casting directors remembering a reject for a different role that came up later. The trick is to be memorable. And if this mad, bad and dangerous day has taught me anything, it's that I'm seriously unusual.

'Babes, you're on!' Billie says.

CHAPTER 8

I stand before the panel, wearing a smile I barely feel. Edwina Hirsch sits in the middle, hair piled on top of her head like a three-tiered chocolate fountain, a spine as straight as a javelin, and unblinking cat eyes. The queen of British theatre is holding court. Back in the day, Edwina was a world-class ballerina before she broke her leg then discovered she had a gift for musical theatre. To her right sits Dalton Wright who was in a boyband in the nineties, then had a short run on a soap, before the producers killed his character off after he kept turning up on set drunk. Dude might be relapsing cos his face is flushed and his man-weave is glued on wonky. Completing the judging panel is Ananya Banerjee, a British Bangladeshi journalist who co-hosted a daytime TV show a few years ago before turning to radio. A pink gem glistens above her right nostril, a wide smile simmering beneath it.

'Tell us your name, where you're from and why you think you'd be perfect for the role,' says Edwina, rolling her R's in old-school received pronunciation.

I open my mouth and nothing comes out. *Calm down*, I tell myself. *You got this. Be yourself – that's one job you can't screw up*. I manage the first two, no problem.

'What makes you think you're more special than the other girls we've seen?' presses Dalton.

'Nothing,' I admit. 'Cos everyone's special in their own way. But I think you should pick me cos no one would be more dedicated or committed to the role. 5 a.m. call times? No problem. Last minute script changes? I can learn lines faster than you can write them. I'm a triple threat.' I *can* act, sing and dance but should I mention my vocal struggles with public singing? 'But acting is my number one.'

After rolling his eyes twice, Dalton scribbles something on a pad.

'Cinderella is a girl from the wrong side of town,' I continue. 'With big ambitions but everyone's telling her to remember her place. That could be *me* you're talking about, right there. I got bundles of creative energy but three drama lessons a week ain't enough. I want to do it twenty-four-seven. I need it to *breathe*.' I clutch my ribs, flaring my nostrils. 'No one back home seems to understand that, so I keep ending up in trouble. People take one look at me and they think they know who I am. No one ever gives me a chance.'

'What? People hate you because you're beautiful?' Dalton says sassily, placing his hands under his chin as if serving shade on a platter.

'Don't judge a book by its cover,' I quote back at him. 'Everyone's got a story to tell and sometimes a smile can hide pain and tears.'

'Well,' Ananya says with a kind smile. 'We're giving you that chance now.'

Edwina narrows her eyes. 'Begin.'

Taking a deep breath, I recite Sophocles, feeling the power of the words resonating in my soul, forming tremors in the air that seemed to grow bigger and bigger. In my mind I am Polynices in Ancient Greece, pleading for forgiveness from the family I have wronged.

Ananya nods and smiles broadly, while Dalton looks disappointed. Edwina clears her throat, 'That was . . . different. We've had a surfeit of Juliets and a Miranda or two, but you selected a traditionally male role. What was your thinking behind that?'

I shrug. 'Back in the day, men got the best roles. I figured if I was going to show my range, that'd be the way to go.'

'We're casting for Cinderella not Cinder*fella*,' snipes Dalton.

'Yes, but the winning actor gets to give the character her own unique spin,' replies Ananya.

Edwina taps her upper lip. 'There was something in your delivery just now . . . the degree of guilt and self-flagellation. Of course your diction was terrible. The alveolar trills in particular were quite flat.'

I blush. Not sure what she's on about but ashamed all the same.

'Quite horrendous!' Dalton agrees with relish.

Edwina asks me to move on to my song. 'Now I want you to enter into the mind of Cinderella – the school pariah. Don't play her, *be her*. When words are simply not enough in theatre, we sing. Tell the audience through the power of song exactly how you are feeling.'

'What's your song choice?' asks Ananya.

I shuffle about nervously. 'I . . .' The silence is deafening. 'I couldn't find one. So I wrote my own.'

Edwina nods. 'Begin.'

'Mamma was my guiding light; I'mma preach it.

Daddy taught me wrong from right; Him'ma teach it.

Cancer stole my mum away, can't believe it.

Couldn't live another day, wanna leave it.

So Daddy marries another girl, it hurtin' me.

Stepma come to destroy my world, she workin' me.

Sistas brung twin hearts of stone, dem lurk fo' me.

Soulless clones who yell and moan, dem come fo' me.

Daddy don't believe what's said! Dem lie.

But Daddy did and now he's dead. Man die.

Here I am, all alone. Ask why.

Become a slave in my own home. I'mma cry.

Oh-oh-oh-oh! How I cry—'

The rap breaks me, my emotions so raw, the wounds too deep. I cover my face and start to sob, knowing I've blown it. Somehow I always mess *everything* up.

Applause cuts through my downward spiral, making me double take. Ananya is on her feet shouting, 'Brilliant, brilliant!' and clapping like there's no tomorrow. Dalton is looking seriously sketchy, scribbling away on his pad like he's filing a victim report. Edwina's neck has extended like an alert giraffe.

'It's a big YES from me!' Ananya says grinning, sitting down. 'Did you really write those lyrics yourself?'

Rubbing my eyes, I nod. I feel like I'm back at primary school, blubbing in front of the class cos my life sucks.

Dalton raises his eyebrows and sighs as if blowing an invisible balloon. 'Yeah, not really a fan of gimmicks. It's a cover for a lack of talent, isn't it? The rapping was great and all but this is primarily an acting role and there are thousands of kids in inner city schools who can rap. Nothing special.'

'How can you sit there and say that after we've had samey performances all afternoon?' says Ananya, bristling.

'It's how I feel and I've been in the business long enough to know what I'm talking about.'

'You were in three episodes of *EastEnders* and we all know how that ended!'

'It was called *Rochdalers* and we had creative differences! Happens all the time.'

Edwina sniffs and the bickering promptly stops.

'Salma Hashmi, isn't it?' she asks checking her tablet. I nod, the tears drying on my cheeks. 'I believed *every word*. Thank you for reminding me of the magic of performance.'

I cover my mouth, the tears flowing again. Edwina winks and my heart does a backflip.

CHAPTER 9

'You were fricking awesome!' Billie squeals, hugging me like a gigantic clothes peg.

'You think?' I ask doubtfully. In the two minutes it took me to walk back to the green room, I've come to believe I imagined it all; that Edwina and Ananya weren't really all that impressed and were just being polite.

'Girl, it's in the bag!' Billie squeals, receiving a hail of daggers from the other hopefuls and their furious stage mums.

'Young man, can you keep your voice down?' says a woman in a red-and-white polka-dot print dress. 'My daughter is trying to learn her lines.'

Billie flushes and stutters an apology. Anger flares in my heart for my new friend.

'Sorry, can you not misgender my mate, please?' I snap.

Her daughter looks Billie up and down and stifles a laugh.

'A little bit of make-up does not make a boy a girl. It makes *him* a clown,' the woman says, chuckling.

'It's OK, Salma . . .' Billie says going redder, pulling my sleeve.

'No, it's really not,' I insist, refusing to let it go. 'Can you imagine how hard it is for people to present the way they want without bigots making assumptions? It's they/them not he/him.'

'Don't speak to my mum like that!' snaps the girl. 'How's she supposed to keep up with your LGBT-XYZ nonsense?'

Her mother nods. 'If you're going to invent snowflake terms for yourselves, don't expect the rest of us to keep up. You two would be better off auditioning for *The Rocky Horror Show*.'

A calm, commanding voice surprises us all. 'Don't you speak to my daughter or her friend like that.'

I turn around, my heart in my throat. 'Mum!' *I am so dead.*

Mum gives my arm a squeeze, placing her other hand on Billie's shoulder. 'Life is hard enough for teens without adults bullying them too. I work in A&E and I've seen too many children being brought in, thinking they have no place in the world, because of inconsiderate people like you.'

The stage mum purses her lips. 'Come on,

Florence,' she tells her daughter. 'Let's go practise somewhere we can actually hear ourselves *think*.'

I stare at Mum wondering how she got here, wondering if she's going to kill me, but mostly feeling mad-proud of how fiercely she clapped back.

'Thank you,' Billie tells Mum.

'Not at all, love. Thank *you* for contacting me.'

My eyes cut to Billie, a flash of betrayal grinding my gut.

'I'm sorry,' Billie says, hiding behind spread fingers. 'I knew you were going to be awesome. Your mum needed to see it, so I sent her a text after her number came up on your phone.'

'Mum . . . I can explain . . . I'm sorry . . .' I stammer.

'We can have a long conversation when we get home,' she says. 'You defied me and I'm not happy.'

I cringe, feeling my cheeks flush. 'I know and I feel so bad.'

'I've been so busy with late shifts, I haven't been making time for you. I don't ever want you to feel isolated or that you can't come to me with *anything*. My parents did that to me and I've never forgiven them.' For a moment, her face is hard. 'You matter more to me than any school, head teacher, community or friend. I admit, I was terrified of Auntie Balquis and what she'd think. But you're my daughter, Salma, and I'm always going to be here for you.'

I can't . . . today just became one great big weep fest.

We sit in the corner with sandwiches Mum bought from across the road, waiting for the winner to be announced. Mum's telling Billie a funny story about the time a famous MP ended up with a very embarrassing emergency. He walked into A&E with a carrier bag over his head with a couple of peep holes cut out to hide his identity. I turn my phone back on. It pings like I've hit the jackpot, a ton of messages from Mum when she got off her shift earlier today. Guilt swells in my chest for ever doubting her; for giving up on sharing my dreams just cos she was angry. It'll never happen again.

I spot a message from an unknown number. I'm about to hit DELETE when curiosity gets the better of me.

> Yo! Dis is Imran.
>
> How ur audishun go?
>
> Grl I cant stop thnkn abt ur
>
> big princess jasmin eyes.
>
> X

Not gonna lie: Imran *was* cute — in a scary, gangsta sort of way. But if my date-mare with Tariq has taught me anything, it's to make sure your bae isn't a secret scumbag. I delete the text and block the sexy fool.

Edwina steps into the green room and a hush descends. The moment of truth has arrived. Mum and Billie grab my hands.

'First, we'd like to thank everyone who answered our open casting call. All three judges were extremely impressed by the quality of the candidates and we're sure we'll be seeing more of you in the near future. The acting community is a small one, so familiar faces and networking are part and parcel of the biz.

'After much deliberation we've come to a decision.'

You could cut the tension with a knife. I'm praying so hard the veins in my head must be throbbing like leeches.

'Karen Montague, please step forward.'

A tall redhead rises, her smile as wide as the horizon. I clap enthusiastically but my heart just fell off a cliff. At least she's not a blonde . . . so there's that. Plus, like Edwina said, my alveolar trills were crap. And who ever heard of a rapping Cinderella? What was I thinking? Fairy-tale endings are for the stage, not real life. Facts.

Today my dream didn't come true, but I wouldn't change it for the world. It's been completely crazy and it feels like a million years since I was in Mrs Fossey's office getting excluded. I've reconnected with Mum and now I know she's got my back when it comes to acting. That is a big deal. Auntie Balquis is gonna wage war on us, but Mum's ready for it. I've lost a mate and gained a mate. Losing Muzna is the worst, but Billie's shown that sometimes it's easier just to do what your parents want and Muzna's got that problem too. Life is hard so you pick your battles and hope they're the right ones. Guess I finally understand that life isn't about winning, it's about being brave enough to *try*.

Suddenly Mum and Billie are yanking me out of my seat, babbling in my face. What have I done now? I stare at them in confusion before noticing the entire room is looking at me, including Karen who's holding her hand out. Confused by her enthusiastic smile, I get up and walk over. She clutches my hand, entwining her fingers with mine.

'Two very different yet equally powerful performances,' Edwina tells the rapt room. 'So we're going to arrange a callback for the two of you, if you're up for it?'

I cover my mouth, unable to believe what I am hearing. Karen was a shoo-in; it was all over. Wasn't it?

'Salma's definitely up for it,' Mum says, hugging me from behind. 'I won't let her pass up on an opportunity like this.'

'I wish I had a mum like yours,' Billie whispers on the way out. 'I could tell her I'm non-binary and there's nothing I can do to change it except make myself miserable and bunk school. I could tell her I love her . . . and that I wish she loved me.' Billie's lower lips trembles, their eyes filling with tears. 'Then maybe I wouldn't be on my own.'

I squeeze Billie's hand. 'Mate, you're not.'

Outside the theatre, the air has cooled a bit. Pink

and orange clouds mesh across a deep blue sky, the falling sun reducing the tallest buildings to purple silhouettes, gilding the smaller ones with gold.

Mum's phone rings. She pulls it out, slowly makes a thoughtful face, then stuffs it back in her bag. Going out on a limb, I'm guessing the caller was Auntie Balquis.

On the way to Mum's car, we pass a bus shelter with a digital screen. A mysterious-looking woman on the motion poster is aiming a gun, point blank, at the viewer. There's a flash of light as she pulls the trigger and the bullet strikes the screen, creating the illusion that it shattered, as shards of glass seem to fly out. The name of the movie fills the screen and then the action replays in an endless loop of awesomeness.

'Some day that's going to be you,' Mum whispers, giving me a nudge.

I glance at Billie. 'Can totally see that happening!' they agree.

And just like that, the knot in my stomach, getting tighter and more twisted over the last twenty-four hours, suddenly comes undone. Who knows what the future holds? Success or failure? Happiness or regrets? One thing I do know is that the Salma who wants to be a good daughter and the Salma who wants to be an actor is finally the same person – no more split.

The End

If you enjoyed *SPLIT*, you might enjoy *Children of Blood and Bone*, the first book in the smash-hit *New York Times* bestselling trilogy from Tomi Adeyemi

Read on for a taster of the stunning fantasy that has taken the world by storm.

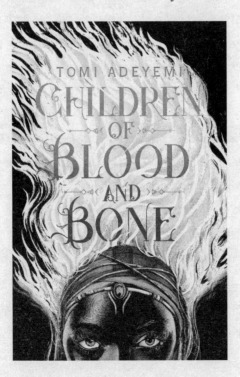

'An epic story of family, love and magic' *Stylist*

Zélie remembers when the soil of Orïsha hummed with magic. When different clans ruled — Burners igniting flames, Tiders beckoning waves, and Zélie's Reaper mother summoning forth souls.

But everything changed the night magic disappeared. Under the orders of a ruthless king, anyone with powers was targeted and killed, leaving Zélie without a mother and her people without hope. Only a few people remain with the power to use magic, and they must remain hidden.

Zélie is one such person. Now she has a chance to bring back magic to her people and strike against the monarchy. With the help of a rogue princess, Zélie must learn to harness her powers and outrun the crown prince, who is hell-bent on eradicating magic for good.

Danger lurks in Orïsha, where strange creatures prowl, and vengeful spirits wait in the waters. Yet the greatest danger may be Zélie herself as she struggles to come to terms with the strength of her magic — and her growing feelings for an enemy.

CHAPTER ONE

ZÉLIE

Pick me.

It's all I can do not to scream. I dig my nails into the marula oak of my staff and squeeze to keep from fidgeting. Beads of sweat drip down my back, but I can't tell if it's from dawn's early heat or from my heart slamming against my chest. Moon after moon I've been passed over.

Today can't be the same.

I tuck a lock of snow-white hair behind my ear and do my best to sit still. As always, Mama Agba makes the selection grueling, staring at each girl just long enough to make us squirm.

Her brows knit in concentration, deepening the creases in her shaved head. With her dark brown skin and muted kaftan, Mama Agba looks like any other elder in the village. You would never guess a woman her age could be so lethal.

"Ahem." Yemi clears her throat at the front of the ahéré, a not-so-subtle reminder that she's already passed this test. She smirks at us as she twirls her hand-carved staff, eager to see which one of us she gets to defeat in our graduation match. Most girls cower at the prospect of facing Yemi, but today I crave it. I've been practicing and I'm ready.

I know I can win.

"Zélie."

Mama Agba's weathered voice breaks through the silence. A collective exhale echoes from the fifteen other girls who weren't chosen. The name bounces around the woven walls of the reed ahéré until I realize Mama Agba's called me.

"Really?"

Mama Agba smacks her lips. "I can choose someone else—"

"No!" I scramble to my feet and bow quickly. "Thank you, Mama. I'm ready."

The sea of brown faces parts as I move through the crowd. With each step, I focus on the way my bare feet drag against the reeds of Mama Agba's floor, testing the friction I'll need to win this match and finally graduate.

When I reach the black mat that marks the arena, Yemi is the first to bow. She waits for me to do the same, but her gaze only stokes the fire in my core. There's no respect in her stance, no promise of a proper fight. She thinks because I'm a divîner, I'm beneath her.

She thinks I'm going to lose.

"*Bow*, Zélie." Though the warning is evident in Mama Agba's voice, I can't bring myself to move. This close to Yemi, the only thing I see is her luscious black hair, her coconut-brown skin, so much lighter than my own. Her complexion carries the soft brown of Orïshans who've never spent a day laboring in the sun, a privileged life funded by hush coin from a father she never met. Some noble who banished his bastard daughter to our village in shame.

I push my shoulders back and thrust my chest forward, straightening though I need to bend. Yemi's features stand out in the crowd of divîners adorned with snow-white hair. Divîners who've been forced to bow to those who look like her time and time again.

"Zélie, do not make me repeat myself."

"But Mama—"

"Bow or leave the ring! You're wasting everyone's time."

With no other choice, I clench my jaw and bow, making Yemi's insufferable smirk blossom. "Was that so hard?" Yemi bows again for good measure. "If you're going to lose, do it with pride."

Muffled giggles break out among the girls, quickly silenced by a sharp wave of Mama Agba's hand. I shoot them a glare before focusing on my opponent.

We'll see who's giggling when I win.

"Take position."

We back up to the edge of the mat and kick our staffs up from the ground. Yemi's sneer disappears as her eyes narrow. Her killer instinct emerges.

We stare each other down, waiting for the signal to begin. I worry Mama Agba'll drag this out forever when at last she shouts.

"Commence!"

And instantly I'm on the defensive.

Before I can even think of striking, Yemi whips around with the speed of a cheetanaire. Her staff swings over her head one moment and at my neck the next. Though the girls behind me gasp, I don't miss a beat.

Yemi may be fast, but I can be faster.

When her staff nears, I arch as far as my back will bend, dodging her attack. I'm still arched when Yemi strikes again, this time slamming her weapon down with the force of a girl twice her size.

I throw myself to the side, rolling across the mat as her staff smacks against its reeds. Yemi rears back to strike again as I struggle to find my footing.

"Zélie," Mama Agba warns, but I don't need her help. In one smooth motion, I roll to my feet and thrust my shaft upward, blocking Yemi's next blow.

Our staffs collide with a loud crack. The reed walls shudder. My weapon is still reverberating from the blow when Yemi pivots to strike at my knees.

I push off my front leg and swing my arms for momentum, cartwheeling in midair. As I flip over her outstretched staff, I see my first opening—my chance to be on the offensive.

"Huh!" I grunt, using the momentum of the aerial to land a strike of my own. *Come on—*

Yemi's staff smacks against mine, stopping my attack before it even starts.

"Patience, Zélie," Mama Agba calls out. "It is not your time to attack. Observe. React. Wait for your opponent to strike."

I stifle my groan but nod, stepping back with my staff. *You'll have your chance*, I coach myself. *Just wait your tur—*

"That's right, Zél." Yemi's voice dips so low only I can hear it. "Listen to Mama Agba. Be a good little maggot."

And there it is.

That word.

That miserable, degrading slur.

Whispered with no regard. Wrapped in that arrogant smirk.

Before I can stop myself, I thrust my staff forward, only a hair from Yemi's gut. I'll take one of Mama Agba's infamous beatings for this later, but the fear in Yemi's eyes is more than worth it.

"Hey!" Though Yemi turns to Mama Agba to intervene, she doesn't have time to complain. I twirl my staff with a speed that makes her eyes widen before launching into another attack.

"This isn't the exercise!" Yemi shrieks, jumping to evade my strike at her knees. "Mama—"

"Must she fight your battles for you?" I laugh. "Come on, Yem. If you're going to lose, do it with *pride*!"

Rage flashes in Yemi's eyes like a bull-horned lionaire ready to pounce. She clenches her staff with a vengeance.

Now the real fight begins.

The walls of Mama Agba's ahéré hum as our staffs smack again and again. We trade blow for blow in search of an opening, a chance to land that crucial strike. I see an opportunity when—

"*Ugh!*"

I stumble back and hunch over, wheezing as nausea climbs up my throat. For a moment I worry Yemi's crushed my ribs, but the ache in my abdomen quells that fear.

"Halt—"

"No!" I interrupt Mama Agba, voice hoarse. I force air into my lungs and use my staff to stand up straight. "I'm okay."

I'm not done yet.

"Zélie—" Mama starts, but Yemi doesn't wait for her to finish. She speeds toward me hot with fury, her staff only a finger's breadth from my head. As she rears back to attack, I spin out of her range. Before she can pivot, I whip around, ramming my staff into her sternum.

"*Ah!*" Yemi gasps. Her face contorts in pain and shock as she reels backward from my blow. No one's ever struck her in one of Mama Agba's battles. She doesn't know how it feels.

Before she can recover, I spin and thrust my staff into her stomach. I'm about to deliver the final blow when the russet sheets covering the ahéré's entrance fly open.

Bisi runs through the doorway, her white hair flying behind her. Her small chest heaves up and down as she locks eyes with Mama Agba.

"What is it?" Mama asks.

Tears gather in Bisi's eyes. "I'm sorry," she whimpers, "I fell asleep, I—I wasn't—"

"Spit it out, child!"

"They're coming!" Bisi finally exclaims. "They're close, they're almost here!"

For a moment I can't breathe. I don't think anyone can. Fear paralyzes every inch of our beings.

Then the will to survive takes over.

"Quickly," Mama Agba hisses. "We don't have much time!"

I pull Yemi to her feet. She's still wheezing, but there's no time to make sure she's okay. I grab her staff and rush to collect the others.

The ahéré erupts in a blur of chaos as everyone races to hide the truth. Meters of bright fabric fly through the air. An army of reed mannequins rises. With so much happening at once, there's no way of knowing whether we'll hide everything in time. All I can do is focus on my task: shoving each staff under the arena mat where they can't be seen.

As I finish, Yemi thrusts a wooden needle into my hands. I'm still running to my designated station when the sheets covering the ahéré entrance open again.

"Zélie!" Mama Agba barks.

I freeze. Every eye in the ahéré turns to me. Before I can speak, Mama Agba slaps the back of my head; a sting only she can summon tears down my spine.

"Stay at your station," she snaps. "You need all the practice you can get."

"Mama Agba, I . . ."

She leans in as my pulse races, eyes glimmering with the truth.

A distraction . . .

A way to buy us time.

"I'm sorry, Mama Agba. Forgive me."

"Just get back to your station."

I bite back a smile and bow my head in apology, sweeping low enough to survey the guards who entered. Like most soldiers in Orïsha, the shorter of the two has a complexion that matches Yemi's: brown like worn leather, framed with thick black hair. Though we're only young girls, he keeps his hand on the pommel of his sword. His grip tightens, as if at any moment one of us could strike.

The other guard stands tall, solemn and serious, much darker than his counterpart. He stays near the entrance, eyes focused on the ground. Perhaps he has the decency to feel shame for whatever it is they're about to do.

Both men flaunt the royal seal of King Saran, stark on their iron breastplates. Just a glance at the ornate snow leopanaire makes my stomach clench, a harsh reminder of the monarch who sent them.

I make a show of sulking back to my reed mannequin, legs nearly collapsing in relief. What once resembled an arena now plays the convincing part of a seamstress's shop. Bright tribal fabric adorns the mannequins in front of each girl, cut and pinned in Mama Agba's signature patterns. We stitch the hems of the same dashikis we've been stitching for years, sewing in silence as we wait for the guards to go away.

Mama Agba travels up and down the rows of girls, inspecting the work of her apprentices. Despite my nerves, I grin as she makes the guards wait, refusing to acknowledge their unwelcome presence.

"Is there something I can help you with?" she finally asks.

"Tax time," the darker guard grunts. "Pay up."

Mama Agba's face drops like the heat at night. "I paid my taxes last week."

"This isn't a trade tax." The other guard's gaze combs over all the divîners with long white hair. "Maggot rates went up. Since you've got so many, so have yours."

Of course. I grip the fabric on my mannequin so hard my fists ache.

It's not enough for the king to keep the diviners down. He has to break anyone who tries to help us.

My jaw clenches as I try to block out the guard, to block out the way *maggot* stung from his lips. It doesn't matter that we'll never become the maji we were meant to be. In their eyes we're still maggots.

That's all they'll ever see.

Mama Agba's mouth presses into a tight line. There's no way she has the coin to spare. "You already raised the diviner tax last moon," she argues. "And the moon before that."

The lighter guard steps forward, reaching for his sword, ready to strike at the first sign of defiance. "Maybe you shouldn't keep company with maggots."

"Maybe you should stop robbing us."

The words spill out of me before I can stop them. The room holds its breath. Mama Agba goes rigid, dark eyes begging me to be quiet.

"Diviners aren't making more coin. Where do you expect these new taxes to come from?" I ask. "You can't just raise the rates again and again. If you keep raising them, we can't pay!"

The guard saunters over in a way that makes me itch for my staff. With the right blow I could knock him off his feet; with the right thrust I could crush his throat.

For the first time I realize that the guard doesn't wield an ordinary sword. His black blade gleams in his sheath, a metal more precious than gold.

Majacite . . .

A weaponized alloy forged by King Saran before the Raid. Created to weaken our magic and burn through our flesh.

Just like the black chain they wrapped around Mama's neck.

A powerful maji could fight through its influence, but the rare metal is debilitating for most of us. Though I have no magic to suppress, the proximity of the majacite blade still pricks at my skin as the guard boxes me in.

"You would do well to keep your mouth shut, little girl."

And he's right. I should. Keep my mouth shut, swallow my rage. Live to see another day.

But when he's this close to my face, it's all I can do not to jam my sewing needle into his beady brown eye. Maybe I should be quiet.

Or maybe he should die.

"*You* sh—"

Mama Agba shoves me aside with so much force I tumble to the ground.

"Here," she interrupts with a handful of coins. "Just take it."

"Mama, don't—"

She whips around with a glare that turns my body to stone. I shut my mouth and crawl to my feet, shrinking into the patterned cloth of my mannequin.

Coins jingle as the guard counts the bronze pieces placed into his palm. He lets out a grunt when he finishes. "It's not enough."

"It has to be," Mama Agba says, desperation breaking into her voice. "This is it. This is everything I have."

Hatred simmers beneath my skin, prickling sharp and hot. This isn't right. Mama Agba shouldn't have to beg. I lift my gaze and catch the guard's eye. A mistake. Before I can turn away or mask my disgust, he grabs me by the hair.

"Ah!" I cry out as pain lances through my skull. In an instant the guard slams me to the ground facedown, knocking the breath from my throat.

"You may not have any money." The guard digs into my back with his knee. "But you sure have your fair share of maggots." He grips my thigh with a rough hand. "I'll start with this one."

My skin grows hot as I gasp for breath, clenching my hands to hide the trembling. I want to scream, to break every bone in his body, but with each second I wither. His touch erases everything I am, everything I've fought so hard to become.

In this moment I'm that little girl again, helpless as the soldier drags my mother away.

"That's enough." Mama Agba pushes the guard back and pulls me to her chest, snarling like a bull-horned lionaire protecting her cub. "You have my coin and that's all you're getting. Leave. Now."

The guard's anger boils at her audacity. He moves to unsheathe his sword, but the other guard holds him back.

"Come on. We've got to cover the village by dusk."

Though the darker guard keeps his voice light, his jaw sets in a tight line. Maybe in our faces he sees a mother or sister, a reminder of some-one he'd want to protect.

The other soldier is still for a moment, so still I don't know what he'll do. Eventually he unhands his sword, cutting instead with his glare. "Teach these maggots to stay in line," he warns Mama Agba. "Or I will."

His gaze shifts to me; though my body drips with sweat, my insides freeze. The guard runs his eyes up and down my frame, a warning of what he can take.

Try it, I want to snap, but my mouth is too dry to speak. We stand in silence until the guards exit and the stomping of their metal-soled boots fades away.

Mama Agba's strength disappears like a candle blown out by the wind. She grabs on to a mannequin for support, the lethal warrior I know diminishing into a frail, old stranger.

"Mama . . ."

I move to help her, but she slaps my hand away. "*Òdè!*"

Fool, she scolds me in Yoruba, the maji tongue outlawed after the

Raid. I haven't heard our language in so long, it takes me a few moments to remember what the word even means.

"What in the gods' names is wrong with you?"

Once again, every eye in the ahéré is on me. Even little Bisi stares me down. But how can Mama Agba yell at me? How is this my fault when those crooked guards are the thieves?

"I was trying to protect you."

"Protect me?" Mama Agba repeats. "You knew your lip wouldn't change a damn thing. You could've gotten all of us killed!"

I stumble, taken aback by the harshness of her words. I've never seen such disappointment in her eyes.

"If I can't fight them, why are we here?" My voice cracks, but I choke down my tears. "What's the point of training if we can't protect ourselves? Why do this if we can't protect you?"

"For gods' sakes, *think*, Zélie. Think about someone other than yourself! Who would protect your father if you hurt those men? Who would keep Tzain safe when the guards come for blood?"

I open my mouth to retort, but there's nothing I can say. She's right. Even if I took down a few guards, I couldn't take on the whole army. Sooner or later they would find me.

Sooner or later they would break the people I love.

"Mama Agba?" Bisi's voice shrinks, small like a mouse. She clings to Yemi's draped pants as tears well in her eyes. "Why do they hate us?"

A weariness settles on Mama's frame. She opens her arms to Bisi. "They don't hate you, my child. They hate what you were meant to become."

Bisi buries herself inside the fabric of Mama's kaftan, muffling her sobs. As she cries, Mama Agba surveys the room, seeing all the tears the other girls hold back.

"Zélie asked why we are here. It's a valid question. We often talk of

11

how you must fight, but we never talk about why." Mama sets Bisi down and motions for Yemi to bring her a stool. "You girls have to remember that the world wasn't always like this. There was a time when everyone was on the same side."

As Mama Agba settles herself onto the chair, the girls gather around, eager to listen. Each day, Mama's lessons end with a tale or fable, a teaching from another time. Normally I would push myself to the front to savor each word. Today I stay on the outskirts, too ashamed to get close.

Mama Agba rubs her hands together, slow and methodical. Despite everything that's happened, a thin smile hangs on her lips, a smile only one tale can summon. Unable to resist, I step in closer, pushing past a few girls. This is our story. Our history.

A truth the king tried to bury with our dead.

"In the beginning, Orïsha was a land where the rare and sacred maji thrived. Each of the ten clans was gifted by the gods above and given a different power over the land. There were maji who could control water, others who commanded fire. There were maji with the power to read minds, maji who could even peer through time!"

Though we've all heard this story at one point or another—from Mama Agba, from parents we no longer have—hearing it again doesn't take the wonder away from its words. Our eyes light up as Mama Agba describes maji with the gift of healing and the ability to cause disease. We lean in when she speaks of maji who tamed the wild beasts of the land, of maji who wielded light and darkness in the palms of their hands.

"Each maji was born with white hair, the sign of the gods' touch. They used their gifts to care for the people of Orïsha and were revered throughout the nation. But not everyone was gifted by the gods." Mama Agba gestures around the room. "Because of this, every time new maji were born, entire provinces rejoiced, celebrating at the first sight of their white coils. The chosen children couldn't do magic before they turned

12

thirteen, so until their powers manifested, they were called the *ibawi*, 'the divine.'"

Bisi lifts her chin and smiles, remembering the origin of our divîner title. Mama Agba reaches down and tugs on a strand of her white hair, a marker we've all been taught to hide.

"The maji rose throughout Orïsha, becoming the first kings and queens. In that time everyone knew peace, but that peace didn't last. Those in power began to abuse their magic, and as punishment, the gods stripped them of their gifts. When the magic leached from their blood, their white hair disappeared as a sign of their sin. Over generations, love of the maji turned into fear. Fear turned into hate. Hate transformed into violence, a desire to wipe the maji away."

The room dims in the echo of Mama Agba's words. We all know what comes next; the night we never speak of, the night we will never be able to forget.

"Until that night the maji were able to survive because they used their powers to defend themselves. But eleven years ago, magic disappeared. Only the gods know why." Mama Agba shuts her eyes and releases a heavy sigh. "One day magic *breathed*. The next, it died."

Only the gods know why?

Out of respect for Mama Agba, I bite back my words. She speaks the way all adults who lived through the Raid talk. Resigned, like the gods took magic to punish us, or they simply had a change of heart.

Deep down, I know the truth. I knew it the moment I saw the maji of Ibadan in chains. The gods died with our magic.

They're never coming back.

"On that fateful day, King Saran didn't hesitate," Mama Agba continues. "He used the maji's moment of weakness to strike."

I close my eyes, fighting back the tears that want to fall. The chain they jerked around Mama's neck. The blood dripping into the dirt.

13

The silent memories of the Raid fill the reed hut, drenching the air with grief.

All of us lost the maji members of our families that night.

Mama Agba sighs and stands up, gathering the strength we all know. She looks over every girl in the room like a general inspecting her troops.

"I teach the way of the staff to any girl who wants to learn, because in this world there will always be men who wish you harm. But I started this training for the divîners, for all the children of the fallen maji. Though your ability to become maji has disappeared, the hatred and violence toward you remains. That is why we are here. That is why we train."

With a sharp flick, Mama removes her own compacted staff and smacks it against the floor. "Your opponents carry swords. Why do I train you in the art of the staff?"

Our voices echo the mantra Mama Agba has made us repeat time and time again. "It avoids rather than hurts, it hurts rather than maims, it maims rather than kills—the staff does not destroy."

"I teach you to be warriors in the garden so you will never be gardeners in the war. I give you the strength to fight, but you all must learn the strength of restraint." Mama turns to me, shoulders pinned back. "You must protect those who can't defend themselves. That is the way of the staff."

The girls nod, but all I can do is stare at the floor. Once again, I've almost ruined everything. Once again, I've let people down.

"Alright," Mama Agba sighs. "That's enough for today. Gather your things. We'll pick up where we left off tomorrow."

The girls file out of the hut, grateful to escape. I try to do the same, but Mama Agba's wrinkled hand grips my shoulder.

"Mama—"

"Silence," she orders. The last of the girls give me sympathetic looks.

They rub their behinds, probably calculating how many lashes my own is about to get.

Twenty for ignoring the exercise . . . fifty for speaking out of turn . . . a hundred for almost getting us killed . . .

No. A hundred would be far too generous.

I stifle a sigh and brace myself for the sting. *It'll be quick*, I coach myself. *It'll be over before it—*

"Sit, Zélie."

Mama Agba hands me a cup of tea and pours one for herself. The sweet scent wafts into my nose as the cup's warmth heats my hands.

I scrunch my eyebrows. "Did you poison this?"

The corners of Mama Agba's lips twitch, but she hides her amusement behind a stern face. I hide my own with a sip of the tea, savoring the splash of honey on my tongue. I turn the cup in my hands and finger the lavender beads embedded in its rim. Mama had a cup like this—its beads were silver, decorated in honor of Oya, the Goddess of Life and Death.

For a moment the memory distracts me from Mama Agba's disappointment, but as the tea's flavor fades, the sour taste of guilt seeps back in. She shouldn't have to go through this. Not for a divîner like me.

"I'm sorry." I pick at the beads along the cup to avoid looking up. "I know . . . I know I don't make things easy for you."

Like Yemi, Mama Agba is a kosidán, an Orïshan who doesn't have the potential to do magic. Before the Raid we believed the gods chose who was born a divîner and who wasn't, but now that magic's gone, I don't understand why the distinction matters.

Free of the white hair of divîners, Mama Agba could blend in with the other Orïshans, avoid the guards' torture. If she didn't associate with us, the guards might not bother her at all.

Part of me wishes she would abandon us, spare herself the pain.

With her tailoring skills, she could probably become a merchant, get her fair share of coin instead of having them all ripped away.

"You're starting to look more like her, did you know that?" Mama Agba takes a small sip of her tea and smiles. "The resemblance is frightening when you yell. You inherited her rage."

My mouth falls open; Mama Agba doesn't like to talk of those we've lost.

Few of us do.

I hide my surprise with another taste of tea and nod. "I know."

I don't remember when it happened, but the shift in Baba was undeniable. He stopped meeting my eyes, unable to look at me without seeing the face of his murdered wife.

"That's good." Mama Agba's smile falters into a frown. "You were just a child during the Raid. I worried you'd forget."

"I couldn't if I tried." Not when Mama had a face like the sun.

It's that face I try to remember.

Not the corpse with blood trickling down her neck.

"I know you fight for her." Mama Agba runs her hand through my white hair. "But the king is ruthless, Zélie. He would sooner have the entire kingdom slaughtered than tolerate divîner dissent. When your opponent has no honor, you must fight in different ways, smarter ways."

"Does one of those ways include smacking those bastards with my staff?"

Mama Agba chuckles, skin crinkling around her mahogany eyes. "Just promise me you'll be careful. Promise you'll choose the right moment to fight."

I grab Mama Agba's hands and bow my head, diving deep to show my respect. "I promise, Mama. I won't let you down again."

"Good, because I have something and I don't want to regret showing it to you."

Mama Agba reaches into her kaftan and pulls out a sleek black rod. She gives it a sharp flick. I jump back as the rod expands into a gleaming metal staff.

"Oh my gods," I breathe out, fighting the urge to clutch the masterpiece. Ancient symbols coat every meter of the black metal, each carving reminiscent of a lesson Mama Agba once taught. Like a bee to honey, my eyes find the *akofena* first, the crossed blades, the swords of war. *Courage does not always roar*, she said that day. *Valor does not always shine.* My eyes drift to the *akoma* beside the swords next, the heart of patience and tolerance. On that day . . . I'm almost positive I got a beating that day.

Each symbol takes me back to another lesson, another story, another wisdom. I look at Mama, waiting. Is this a gift or what she'll use to beat me?

"Here." She places the smooth metal in my hand. Immediately, I sense its power. Iron-lined . . . weighted to crack skulls.

"Is this really happening?"

Mama nods. "You fought like a warrior today. You deserve to graduate."

I rise to twirl the staff and marvel at its strength. The metal cuts through the air like a knife, more lethal than any oak staff I've ever carved.

"Do you remember what I told you when we first started training?"

I nod and mimic Mama Agba's tired voice. "'*If you're going to pick fights with the guards, you better learn how to win.*'"

Though she slaps me over the head, her hearty laughter echoes against the reed walls. I hand her the staff and she rams it into the ground; the weapon collapses back into a metal rod.

"You know how to win," she says. "Just make sure you know when to fight."

Pride and honor and pain swirl in my chest when Mama Agba places the staff back into my palm. Not trusting myself to speak, I wrap my hands around her waist and inhale the familiar smell of freshly washed fabric and sweet tea.

Though Mama Agba stiffens at first, she holds me tight, squeezing away the pain. She pulls back to say more, but stops as the sheets of the ahéré open again.

I grab the metal rod, prepared to flick until I recognize my older brother, Tzain, standing in the entrance. The reed hut instantly shrinks in his massive presence, all muscle and strain. Tendons bulge against his dark skin. Sweat rains from his black hair down his forehead. His eyes catch mine and a sharp pressure clamps my heart.

"It's Baba."

'A perspective long overdue in British fiction'

Alex Wheatle, author of *Crongton Knights*

'FUNNY, ANGRY, POWERFUL'
PATRICE LAWRENCE,
AWARD-WINNING
AUTHOR OF
ORANGEBOY

I AM THUNDER
AND I WON'T KEEP QUIET

KICK THE MOON

'A book steeped in drama and empathy'

Nikesh Shukla, author of *Run Riot*

MUHAMMAD KHAN
FROM THE AUTHOR OF THE CRITICALLY-ACCLAIMED *I AM THUNDER*

ABOUT THE AUTHOR

Muhammad Khan is an engineer, a secondary-school maths teacher, and a YA author! He takes his inspiration from the children he teaches, as well as his own upbringing as a British-born Pakistani. He lives in South London and has an MA in Creative Writing from St Mary's. His debut novel *I Am Thunder* was shortlisted for the 2019 YA Book Prize, has won the 2019 Branford Boase First Novel Award, the 2018 Great Reads Award and a number of regional awards. His second novel, *Kick the Moon*, nominated for the 2020 Carnegie Medal is also published by Macmillan Children's Books and *Mark My Words* will be published in summer 2020.

#ReadingisPower

Whatever the time of day, morning, noon or night, there's always time to discover and share stories. You can . . .

1 PAY A VISIT to your LOCAL BOOKSHOP

A treasure trove of books to browse and choose, you'll also find excellent tips and reading recommendations from helpful booksellers, and lots of book-themed events to enjoy.

FIND YOUR LOCAL BOOKSHOP: booksellers.org.uk/ bookshopsearch

2 JOIN your LOCAL LIBRARY

So many books to browse and borrow – entirely for free! Get advice on what to read next, and take part in their brilliant free activities.

FIND YOUR LOCAL LIBRARY: gov.uk/local-library -services/

3 GO TO the WORLD BOOK DAY WEBSITE

If you need inspiration, reading and writing tips, ideas or resources, **worldbookday.com** is packed with fun and exciting podcasts, videos, activities, interviews with your favourite authors and illustrators, all the latest book news and much more.

Celebrate stories. Love reading.

READING IS POWER

- What's the **GREATEST BOOK** you've ever read, the most **POWERFUL STORY** ever told?

- Which **AUTHOR** speaks to you the loudest, who is the **CHARACTER** that **STUCK IN YOUR HEAD** long after you put the book down?

- Which **ILLUSTRATORS** enchant you and make you want to pick up a pen yourself?

- How do you get your **BOOKISH** fix? Downloaded to your phone or do you prefer the feel of a book in your hands?

How do *you* share stories?

Here at World Book Day, **we celebrate books in all their glory and guises**, we love to **think and talk about books**. Did you know we are a **charity**, here to bring books, your favourite **authors and illustrators** and much more to readers like you?

We believe **BOOKS AND READING ARE A GIFT,** and this book is our gift to **YOU.**

#ShareAStory today, in celebration of all the books you love